M000031726

"But why is Don Carlos continuing his battle when both governments want peace?" I asked the old man. I had asked Hawk and I had even asked the President that same question. Their answers had been couched in protocol, political speculation, rumor. The old man's answer was the only true one.

"Because he is a man of Satan, not a man of God."

What couldn't be true was the old man's description of Don Carlos Italla. A giant of seven feet, a mountainous specimen of three hundred pounds, eyes like ingots of burning phosphorous, hands that could shred stainless steel slabs. A fury of a monster with a booming voice like the rumble of thunder. . .

It couldn't be true. . .

NICK CARTER IS IT!

"Nick Carter out-Bonds James Bond."
—*Buffalo Evening News*

"Nick Carter is America's #1 espionage agent."
—*Variety*

"Nick Carter is razor-sharp suspense."
—*King Features*

"Nick Carter is extraordinarily big."
—*Bestsellers*

"Nick Carter has attracted an army of addicted readers . . . the books are fast, have plenty of action and just the right degree of sex . . . Nick Carter is the American James Bond, suave, sophisticated, a killer with both the ladies and the enemy."
—*The New York Times*

*Dedicated to the men of the
Secret Services of the
United States of America*

NICK CARTER

WAR FROM THE CLOUDS

CHARTER
NEW YORK

A DIVISION OF CHARTER COMMUNICATIONS INC.
A GROSSET & DUNLAP COMPANY

WAR FROM THE CLOUDS

Copyright © 1980 by Condé Nast Publications, Inc.
All rights reserved. No part of this book may be reproduced in
any form or by any means, except for the inclusion of brief
quotations in a review, without permission in writing from the
publisher.

All characters in this book are fictitious. Any resemblance to
actual persons, living or dead, is purely coincidental.

A Charter Original.

"Nick Carter" is a registered trademark of The Conde Nast
Publications, Inc., registered in the United States Patent Office.

First Charter Printing November 1980
Published simultaneously in Canada
Manufactured in the United States of America

2 4 6 8 0 9 5 3 1

CHAPTER 1

He was definitely a Cuban Marine. He had this particular swagger, this incredible poise, even when crabbing across volcanic banks or hacking through jungles or sweating out his guts on mountain trails.

I had followed him for six miles through the night. Across the volcanic bank of Mt. Toro, through a section of the Nicarxa Rain Forest; now he was resting, getting his breath in short, gasping snorts preparatory to making the climb to Alto Arete.

Home of Don Carlos Italla, the wizard of war, the vicious chieftain of guerilla forces that would not let peace come to this beautiful land.

Don Carlos, the monk, the man of God, the religious fanatic whose religion was the taking of lives, the shedding of blood, the stirring of maniacal passions in men who would be far better off at home screwing their wives, tilling their fields, drinking their vino, loving their children.

And the Cuban Marines were the left hand of

this God, this humble monk who loved war above everything and who lived in ultimate protection and seclusion among his monk-brothers in the ancient abbey that occupied the flat top of Alto Arete, three thousand feet above the jungle floor.

It was my job to bring the man down from his mountain lair. To topple the man-God. To eliminate the Cuban Marines, to educate the monk's followers or to kill them, to bring peace once again to Alto Arete and peace to the Reina Valley below that lofty peak.

My name? Nick Carter. My job? For the moment, to topple the man-god named Don Carlos Italla.

"Nick," Hawk had said, "we have put the finishing touches on a peace treaty that will end the long war between Nicarxa and Apalca."

"Are they both willing to sign?" I asked.

In fact, I had not known that Nicarxa and Apalca, two island Republics south of Cuba, had even been at war. But there are, at any given time, perhaps fifteen small wars going on in various parts of the world. It's the big wars that get all the publicity.

"Everyone involved has agreed to it," Hawk said. "Except for Don Carlos Italla. He is a violent enemy of the Nicarxan power structure. Religious differences, mostly, but there's a rumor that someone in the country once did something rather atrocious to him or his family. I don't know the details. I do know that Don Carlos must be shown the light. Think you can handle it, Nick?"

"I certainly can, sir."

If I had known what I later learned, I probably wouldn't have said anything so abysmally foolish.

I don't know what I would have told the man, but it would not have been a definite, foolish, braggadocio like that.

I also knew that I had a great deal more to learn, all of it bad for our side. All I knew for certain (which was more than I wanted to know once I had learned it) was that Don Carlos and his closest lieutenants were on top of Alto Arete, which I could now see in the distance, dark clouds hovering around its great, lumpy peak. They were armed to the teeth. The only way up was by a narrow, winding mountain trail that left enormous gaps missing from its path. The trail was guarded from bottom to top.

What I didn't know was how many guards were on location, top or bottom. I also didn't know if other defenses were on the mountain—minefields, electrified fences, snake pits, guard dogs, that sort of thing.

The Cuban Marine was going to tell me what I didn't know, only he didn't know yet that he was going to tell me.

He was only a hundred yards ahead of me now. We were still two miles from the base of Alto Arete, where the trail began its vertical climb to the top, still swathed in cumulus clouds.

I increased my pace, sweating like a eunuch with an erection, narrowing the distance between us. Ahead was a small farmhouse, nestled in the foothills, sheep grazing in a meadow beside a meandering stream. The Cuban, as cool as viewer reaction to a new sit-com television program, veered from the trail and walked with uncanny grace down toward the farmhouse.

I waited until he had crossed the stream, then I

checked my weaponry. Strapped to the small of my
back was Wilhelmina, the big, booming Luger that
had no notches for kills. If I had begun to notch my
pistol, Wilhelmina would have disappeared long
ago in a mass of filings.

There was Pierre, my admittedly old-fashioned
gas bomb, but effective as ever in this world of
modern chemicals, potions, drugs and hallucinogens
spurted from aerosol cans. He was cool and calm
in his tiny lamb's wool pouch right behind my testicles. All three were precious to me.

Last, but sometimes first to be used, was Hugo,
my razor-sharp stiletto that is always in a sheath on
my wrist. Always, that is, except when in use.
Sometimes, though, I have to use more primitive
weapons. They are also quite effective, even in this
modern world. I call them "hands."

I stood near the trail, behind a banana tree,
keeping an eye out above for the massive scorpions
that love green bananas, and watched the Cuban
disappear into shadows beside the farmhouse. I
knew where he was. When the door opened and
mellow light streaked out into the softly-moonlit
night, it was confirmed. He was standing on the
farmer's porch and I figured he had stopped for a
drink of water, or perhaps vino.

I was wrong.

The feminine scream that rent the quiet jungle
night told me one thing, and one only. The farmer
had a daughter. The Cuban knew about her. He
had stopped for fun and frolic, and she was not
really very interested.

The Cuban Marine's obvious poise had failed to
charm the lass.

Even as I dashed noiselessly down the path toward the stream, I triggered the release to snap Hugo into my hand. Time was important, but silence was vital. There was a whole detachment of Cuban Marines two miles ahead. One bark from Wilhelmina and the sound would ricochet off Alto Arete, sending the whole damned detachment down the trail in quadruple time.

Screams, especially feminine ones, didn't send them crashing out of their tents. Feminine screams had been rather commonplace in this valley since Don Carlos Italla had brought in the Cubans.

They would never become commonplace with me.

My boss, David Hawk, once told me: "Nick, you'll never fall prey to the real enemy. No man, however monstrous, however vicious, however powerful, will ever best you. You'll get yours, my boy, on the trail of a lady's petticoat."

The ladies I fool around with—and occasionally save—haven't worn petticoats in fifty years, but Hawk is a bit old-fashioned.

I got over the stream without even getting my shoes wet. Another scream, muffled by the closed door, cracked into the night. A wild, frightened bird from a banana tree responded with a horrible shriek. Then silence. So silent that I could hear the husky trickling of the stream behind me.

I disappeared into the shadows, but avoided the front porch. The first three windows produced nothing of interest—an overturned chair, a smashed pitcher, a rumpled rug, all indicating signs of struggle in the family parlor. At the fourth window, I saw the farmer and his wife huddling on their bed. They had to huddle; they were tied together.

The fifth window said it all.

The Cuban had stripped the girl, who was one hell of a ripe-looking young thing, and she was cowering naked on her narrow cot. Her black hair fell in cascades about her tear-stained face, covering most of her nubile breasts. She was trying to cover herself, but her slender brown hands couldn't handle all the chores at once.

The Cuban Marine was slipping off his pants, his tongue out, his bulging eyes taking in the view of nipples, creamy breast, pubic hair, rounded little belly, the long expanses of thigh that glistened enticingly in light from a kerosene lamp.

As the Marine slung his trousers against a far wall and began unbuttoning his tunic, I edged my hands up to the window frame. Hugo was clamped tightly in my teeth. The window wouldn't budge from slight pressure, so I gave it a healthy shove. Nothing.

The tunic was off, going the way of the trousers. The Cuban Marine was a husky one. His light brown muscles rippled in the kerosene lamplight as he whisked off a grimy white tee shirt and snaked his thumbs under the waistband of his shorts and jerked down quickly. His back was to me, so I couldn't tell what was going on in front until I saw the girl's eyes widen. She was staring at his crotch. What she saw brought new terror.

It was then that she gave me the opportunity to act without alarming the local Marine detachment or getting my head blown off. The man's rifle was leaning against the foot of the bed and the girl made a lunge for it.

She moved fast. The Cuban was late in responding, but he flipped away his shorts and dashed for the rifle just as the girl closed her hands on the barrel.

I hit the window frame with the heels of both hands, the lock broke and the window went up with the jerking swiftness of a killer carnival ride.

The girl was squealing, the man roaring, so the sound of the rising window was lost on that. I leaped in headfirst, ducking my head low to bring my feed around. I landed in the middle of the room on my heels and buttocks, then flipped up to my feet. The Cuban, his hands grasping the stock of the rifle, turned abruptly and glared at me, teeth and gums bared like a trapped animal's.

"*Quien es?*" the man hissed in Spanish. "*Que pasa?*"

"Just a little disturbing of the peace," I said, unable to resist that horrible old pun. Too bad he didn't understand English. As it was, I caught a tiny crinkling around the corners of his mouth. By God, he *did* understand English.

I was in my if-you-don't-attack-me, I-won't-attack-you crouch, Hugo glistening in my outstretched right hand.

The girl suddenly let go of the rifle and flipped back on the bed. Another display of streaking goodies until she yanked a sheet up around her.

The Cuban's eyes had followed her. My eyes had followed her. Now we were eyeball-to-eyeball. He had the right end of the rifle. I had the right end of Hugo.

"*Quien es?*" he said again in Spanish, asking me who I was.

"My name is Carter," I said politely, inching Hugo a bit nearer his now flaccid member. "I'm also known as N3, also Killmaster, the *numero uno* agent for AXE. Does that clarify things?"

He began moving his hand toward the trigger guard. His large blue eyes were on my large brown eyes, although both of us were being torn apart by an urge to see what the beauty was doing on the cot.

"Lower the rifle," I said, "or I remove your manhood."

"*No hablo engles*," he said.

If he did speak English. I thought, he's taking one hell of a chance. His manhood was on the line. His hand moved another quarter of an inch on the stock.

I lunged forward. The man leaped backward. The girl screamed. I made a light swipe with the stiletto, drawing only a few drops of blood right at the stump of his penis where it disappeared into crinkly black hair. He yelped in the universal language of pain.

His finger found the trigger and I aimed Hugo to another place. It was a good aim. The vibrating point of the stiletto caught the fingernail and sliced through it as through icing on a baby's birthday cake. I felt the blade grind against bone as I whipped the stiletto up, nearly severing his trigger finger.

The rifle went flying, as I knew it would. The girl screamed again, as I knew she would. The Cuban had both hands on his bleeding manhood, as I knew anyone would.

And it was over. So easy. Talk sense to any man in any language and he'll get your point. Hugo is tops in his field at talking sense and making points.

What I learned during the next few minutes made me sick to my stomach.

After untying the old farm couple and using the ropes to tie up my Cuban jock-commando-makeout artist-Marine, I learned that the people were Jorge and Melina Cortez. The daughter was Elicia, age seventeen. A son, Antonio, age nineteen, had been conscripted into the Italla guerilla band a year ago, hadn't been heard from—or of—since.

Elicia had lost her virginity three months ago when the Cuban Marines arrived. She had lost it the same way she was about to lose her free will tonight. A Marine had stopped by on his way between the village and the garrison, after having seen the girl riding her horse in the fields. Drunk, he had decided to test the wares, had found them suitable and had brazenly told his fellows.

For three months, Elicia had had callers almost nightly. Even though her parents knew the routine and never fought, the routine was always the same. Elicia screamed when a Marine appeared, the Marine tied up the old folks and ripped the girl's clothing from her body.

After three months, she still fought. Her hatreds were gestating like laboratory cultures.

Why didn't the old man get a gun and shoot the next bastard who came to entertain his daughter? Threats, that's why. A roll in the sack would be the least the girl could expect if the old man fought back.

The visits may not have been under the sanction of Don Carlos Italla, but he had been told of them, had said nothing. He needed the Cuban Marines; he didn't need that old farm couple and their lovely daughter.

"But why is Don Carlos continuing his battle

when both governments want peace?" I asked the
old man. I had asked Hawk and I had even asked
the President that same question. Their answers
had been couched in protocol, political guessing,
rumor; much flim-flam. The old man's answer was
the only true answer.

"Because he is a man of Satan, not a man of
God."

What wasn't true, I hoped, was the old man's
description of Don Carlos Italla. A giant of seven
feet, a mountainous specimen of three hundred
pounds, eyes like ingots of burning phosphorous,
hands that could shred stainless steel slabs. A fury
of a monster with a booming voice like the rumble
of thunder.

Obviously, Don Carlos Italla was the local
dragon, a creature to rival Tolkien's Smaug, hidden away on his evil mountaintop where no woman had ever gone, where Satan was welcome, where
wars were planned, but never fought, in clouds.

Well, it was time for a few changes.

If Don Carlos would not come from his cloudy
retreat to wage war with me, I would take war to
him. My brand of war, on my terms.

Wizards and giants and men of Satan have
always given me a royal pain in the ass.

Elicia had gone into shock after the little scrap
between me and her would-be lover. Her mother
bathed her, bundled her up and sat in the back
bedroom rocking her on her lap, singing in a low,
mellow voice of lost Spanish princes and faraway
castles. The proper nursing for children. And she
was a child, not equipped mentally or physically
for the kind of abuse that had come to her from
across the Caribbean.

Anger was building in me with every word the old farmer spoke. And the filthy soldier sat listening to those words, still holding his crotch. I couldn't be cruel enough to tie his hands behind him, but they were tied nonetheless. After listening to the old man, and learning also that this was the third visit for this bastard, I wished I had cut off his hands altogether.

"All right, up," I said, looming above him.

"*No comprendo*," he said, looking up with what I interpreted as disdain.

Good, you son of a bitch, keep it up. I'm only pissed off right now, you just wait until I get mad.

"You understand," I said.

He stood, but I had made a rising gesture with my hands as I talked, so it could have been from that. Maybe he didn't speak English. I knew that my Spanish wasn't adequate for the details I needed from this jocko. In time.

Jorge Melina gave me a lantern to find our way down to the barn. I didn't want him or his wife to see what was to happen next. It's hardly something you'd take to school for show-and-tell day.

The horse, whose name I learned was Pistola, glared at us through huge, frightened eyes as we stumbled into the ramshackle barn. I walked with hard strides, barely containing my anger. I wanted to hit. I mean, really *hit*. My intentions must have been obvious to my Marine friend, because as soon as we hit the barn he began to sing.

CHAPTER TWO

The Marine's name was Luis Pequeno and it was not a pleasure killing him. Killing is never a pleasure, except for the hopelessly insane, even under extreme conditions when your life is threatened. I have never killed without remorse; I hope to God I never do.

What bothered me most was that my life was in no immediate danger from Sgt. Luis Pequeno. But, if I let him live, he would most certainly make his way to his unit and report my activities and purposes in the little island country. At that point, my life wouldn't be worth the sweat off Pistola's shanks.

What Luis Pequeno had told me convinced me of that.

The Cuban contingent, he said, was headed by Col. Ramon Vasco, a man who was every bit as much a maniac as Don Carlos Italla. Colonel Vasco had grown up in New York City, returning to Cuba to join Fidel Castro's revolutionaries in

1957. His experiences in the Cuban "minority sector" of Gotham had built in him a crushing hatred of Americans.

"He has told us repeatedly," Luis said when I had untied him, "that if we find any Americans interfering with our great cause here in Nicarxa we are to disembowel them and feed them to the pigs."

Even worse than Colonel Vasco's grimly-dedicated hatred of Americans were the solid military defenses he had arranged for the protection of Don Carlos and his fellow monks.

Alto Arete, Luis said, spilling his guts the way he had been instructed to spill American guts, was truly impregnable. The trail up the side of Mt. Toro was accessible only by ropes controlled from above. The gaps in the trail were the colonel's idea. He had dynamited them out to create immense chasms, and had established rescue stations above the points where the trail had been blown away.

From above, armed soldiers would ascertain if the traveler was welcome. If so, they would lower ropes and raise the visitor to the next level in the trail. If not, they would drop boulders on the poor sap. And the soldiers were so well hidden in their outposts above the trail that no firepower from below could unseat them.

Even before a traveler could start up the trail, he had to pass through a thousand Cuban Marines bivouacked in a base camp at the foot of Mount Toro. Security was tight here and, so far, no unwelcome visitor had made it past the Marines. Once, though, Luis told me, the soldiers at the first outpost—the first break in the trail—had mistaken a party of Nicarxan diplomats for the enemy and had crushed them all with boulders, then had emptied their Russian XZ47's into their wrinkled corpses.

If an unwanted visitor or enemy should penetrate the Marines and somehow make his way around the breaks in the trail, through bits of sharp metal impregnated with curare, that visitor would be greeted near the top of Alto Arete by a minefield. If he got through that in one piece, he would encounter a high metal fence charged with ten thousand volts of electricity. If, by some insane and perverse twist of reality, he should get over that fence without being fried to a crisp, he would be met by a hundred armed monks and vicious guard dogs infected with rabies.

Attack from the air was equally futile, even if I had access to a fleet of bombers or fighter planes. Computer-controlled antiaircraft guns rimmed the boundaries of Alto Arete. They had already destroyed the total air force of resisting guerillas and had shot down a number of private planes that had ventured near the sacred mountain column.

As if all that news wasn't depressing enough, Sergeant Pequeno went on to say that Don Carlos had plans to start a bloody revolution in just six days. The crazy monk, who was in constant radio contact with his agents in the capital, had arranged to have a group of Apalcan allies visit him on the mountaintop in a few days. If he gained their full support for his revolutionary ideals, he would signal the start of the war. His own guerillas, with the help of the Cubans, would annihilate all government resistance and would even kill the peace commission members already trying to work out a treaty between the two island countries.

After all the dust had cleared, Luis said, Don

Carlos would be the undisputed chieftain of both island nations and would be surrounded only by fanatic believers. Together, under the leadership and guidance of these crackpots, Nicarxa and Apalca would commence a reign of terror, a crusade of conquests that could quite quickly lead the world into its third major conflict.

As far as I knew—and my information came directly from the President of the United States—I was the only American in Nicarxa. And I knew also that I was the only man outside of Don Carlos Italla's gaggle of crackpots who knew of his plans. In short, N3, Killmaster for AXE, was the only man who could stop Don Carlos. Unfortunately, I couldn't do it with the plans and weapons at my disposal. And I certainly couldn't do it if Sgt. Luis Pequeno walked free and told what he knew of me. I already had been exposed to his penchant for singing like a bird of everything he knew.

"Turn around, sergeant," I had said when Luis had finished his incredible tale. "Open the door to the horse's stall and go inside. I'm going to tie you securely and take your uniform. I have plans for it. You'll be safe here. Even the family you terrorized will feed you and bring you water."

There was a smile on the sergeant's face as he entered the stall. Pistola moved aside, her eyes glinting in the lantern light, afraid of this new incursion of her privacy. Luis was convinced of my softness, knowing that all Americans are soft and cannot summon the courage or the viciousness to do what must be done in a tough, troubled world. He felt safe because of that knowledge, and because he knew that his comrades would come by each night to see Elicia, and would free him.

I let those comforting thoughts rattle around in the sergeant's head for a time, feeling that it's bad enough to die with violence, much less with frightened and troubled thoughts. But my stalling wasn't mere stalling.

"One last favor, Sergeant," I said, taking out my notebook and a pen. "I want you to help me draw a map of the fortifications on top of Alto Arete. After that, I'll leave you to sleep and then Senor Cortez will bring you food. Will you help me?"

It took quite a while to get a suitable map drawn. I caught Luis in a number of lies, diversions from his original story, but I was finally convinced that the map was mostly accurate. I pocketed the notebook and pen, and got up. I walked around behind the Marine sergeant and slipped Hugo into my hand.

"I'll be leaving you now, Sergeant," I said softly.

He was turning toward me, a smile broadening on his face, when my hand leapt out and pressed the nerve juncture beside his neck at the top of his right shoulder.

He went instantly unconscious and I moved into the stall, Hugo in my hand. I plunged the stiletto through his ribcage, striking straight at the heart. He felt nothing and he died in a few seconds. I got a shovel and buried him in the stall. I buried him deep.

"Aaaiiiieee!"

Elicia cried out in panic when I entered the house. She was still cradled in her mother's arms. She might have slept, fitfully, but now she was awake and the sight of the Marine's uniform sent her back to the depths of terror.

"It's all right," I said, hastily but softly. "It's all right, Elicia. I'm not the Cuban. I'm the man who saved you from him. I merely need his uniform."

Old Jorge and Melina were the first to come around. When they knew that it was me and not the burly Cuban, huge smiles spread across their wrinkled faces, revealing teeth that had never known a moment of dental hygiene.

"It is as he says, *niña*," the old man said to his daughter. "It is the good man, not the bad one. Where is—what have you done with the soldier?"

I told them. It would have been no good lying to them. Their eyes widened in horror and fright. I had to calm them.

"You don't have to worry about other Marines finding him," I said. "You'd have much greater worries if he were alive. Now, it's a certainty that his buddies will come here looking for him, and for Elicia. It's important that we get you all out of here, to some safe place in the mountains. I'll try—"

"No," Jorge said, shaking his old head vigorously. "Here is where I was born, here is where I will die. You take Elicia to my cousin's house in the hills. She can show you where it is. When the soldiers come, we will pretend ignorance. They will not find the body. If they do, we are ready to die. Please, take our daughter and care for her. Find our son and he will help."

"No," the old woman said, cradling Elicia closer to her ample bosom. "My child stays here."

"*Basta!*" the old man snapped, turning on her. "We deal in our own lives now, old woman. You cannot have all you wish in life. Take Elicia, take her now."

It was settled in that manner. When the Marines came, the old couple would say that the Marine sergeant came, raped Elicia and kidnapped her. A search would be made of the premises, but I'd buried the sergeant well, was wearing his uniform, and the smell of the stable would prevent even well-trained bloodhounds from sniffing out his grave.

Ten minutes later, I retrieved my knapsack hidden near the farm. Leaving my portable radio there, Elicia and I set out on foot in the darkness, heading along narrow trails in the inky blackness of the jungle night. The girl was no longer crying, but she was still terrified—and a part of it was fear of me. I made certain not to touch her as we moved through the night. A few times, we accidentally bumped together and she recoiled as though I were a snake. It was not the happiest of situations.

An hour after we left the house, Elicia came to a stop on a ledge high above the valley. She stopped without warning and I ran smack into her warm, supple body. She didn't recoil. I felt her finger against my lip and heard her low shushing sound.

"Just ahead," she said in a melodic accent that was surprisingly soft in view of her earlier screeching and carrying on, "is an open place where we should be able to see the main encampment. We must be careful not to be seen by them."

We moved slowly forward and, sure enough, entered an open area where we had a clear view of the Reina Valley below; clear, that is, except for the darkness that lay on the land like a black velvet curtain. In the murky distance, I could make out silhouettes of darkened houses, of trees, of the meandering river that ran down from the arroyos and gullies and springs of Mount Toro. There were few lights in the houses. Since the Cubans had come, most of the citizens had imposed a kind of curfew on themselves, afraid to venture out, afraid even of letting the pillaging Marines know that they were alive.

I brought my gaze upward and saw a dark column rising into the sky. It was Alto Arete and, from the lookout, the mountain column looked like an enormous chimney rising from Mount Toro. I hadn't seen Alto Arete from this vantage point before. It was imposing, impressive and, worse than all, frightening and impregnable.

Elicia tugged at my sleeve (the sergeant's sleeve, actually) and brought me nearer the sharp edge of the ledge. "To the left," she said, "where you see the glow of light."

I leaned forward, aware that my toes in Luis Pequeno's big combat boots were jutting out into space, and saw the glow, then what was causing it. Tucked away in a little valley off the main valley were dozens of campfires. They stretched up the narrow hollow and around the base of the mountain, like an electric necklace around an ebony neck. It was the thousand Marines, guarding the advances to the main trail up to Alto Arete.

In that moment, I gave thanks to the intuitive reasoning that had put me on the trail of the Cuban Marine. If I hadn't followed him, I wouldn't have found the Cortez family and this girl. Without the girl, I'd never had found this safe trail up the mountain opposite Mount Toro. Without this safe trail, I would have stumbled headlong into that encampment of Marines and would have been disemboweled and fed to the pigs. Or to those rabid dogs up on top.

"Beyond that encampment," Elicia said in that same soft, tuneful voice, "is the encampment of the guerillas supporting Don Carlos. None of us dares go near either encampment, but I have watched with my horse from this point. I am certain that Antonio is down there, with the other guerillas.

"But he's so close to home," I said. "Why wouldn't he break away and come back to his family?"

I could only guess at the expression on her face. I knew she was staring at me as though I were the dumbest gringo who ever lived.

"Deserters are shot," she said. "So are their families, including cousins and those who have married into the families."

"Sweet bunch," I muttered. "Okay, let's get you to your cousin's house, then I'm coming back here to wait for daylight."

"Why would you do that? You can stay with my cousin as well."

"I can't stay anywhere, Elicia. I didn't come all the way down here to hide."

"All right," she said, touching my arm again. I was starting to like that. "I will not hide either. Let us both wait for daylight."

There was no time to explain to her that I planned to figure out the best way to infiltrate that Marine encampment, as Sgt. Luis Pequeno, or that she would only be in the way of my progress. We were hours away from her cousin's house, considering how long it had taken us to reach this point from her parent's farm. I took her arm and pulled her away from the ledge. She didn't recoil from my touch.

"We'll do it my way," I said. "And that means

getting you to safety and me coming back here alone."

"Everybody bosses the Nicarxans," she said almost sullenly. Then, she sighed. In the mellow glow from the Marine's campfires, I could have sworn that I saw a smile on her face. This time, the smile said, she didn't mind being bossed by an outsider.

It took three hours to get her to her cousin's house, actually a hut on Mount Toro's northern slopes. We had crossed and recrossed the valley, and the Reina River, so many times that I lost my way and doubted that I would ever make it back to that lookout point.

As we stood on the dusty road leading to the hut where Elicia would hide, she moved close to me. Her breath smelled of orange blossoms and I wondered how she had managed that, considering the lack of toothbrushes and toothpaste in her parents' home. She rummaged in a pocket and pressed a gold chain and locket into my hand.

"Antonio gave this to me on my sixteenth birthday," she said, "Give it to him and he will know that you are our friend."

"Maybe not," I said, always the doubting Thomas. "He might think I stole it from you. Or took it by force."

"No," she said. "Before we left my parent's house, I folded a note into the locket."

I started to object, recalling her reluctance to go with me, remembering how she had recoiled from my touch on the trail. And then I knew. She had trusted me from the beginning, but her memories of what those Marines had been doing to her was so fresh in her mind that she would have recoiled from the touch of any male. The fact that she had warmed to me at all was proof enough that the memories were fading as the trust built in her.

I thought about kissing her goodbye then, but discarded the idea. There is such a thing as pushing your luck. Even as I was thinking this, she stood on tiptoe, found my face in the darkness and kissed me soundly and sweetly on the lips.

And then, like a wraith or a shadow, she was gone and I stood like an adolescent lover on the dirt road following her body with my imagination. The strains of the lovely old song, "On the Street Where You Live" raced through my mind.

It was with great reluctance that I turned to retrace my steps to the ledge above the Marine encampment.

Light was just beginning to filter down on the mountains when I made it back to the lookout point Elicia had shown me. I snuggled close to the ground and watched the encampment as dawn increased. When there was sufficient light, I took my binoculars from my knapsack, studied the layout of the Marine detachment and could find no indications of which company was bivouacked where. Sergeant Pequeno had told me that he was in the Baker Company of the second battalion. I would do everything possible to avoid that battalion: even if I could pass as the dead sergeant, I had no intentions of being shot for desertion. Luis was already several hours AWOL.

But the uniform and my use of Spanish would at least get me into the encampment without drawing undue suspicion. After that, I should have no trouble finding out precisely where the guerillas were encamped, no trouble walking there to make discreet enquiries about one Antonio Cortez.

Or so I thought.

I again hid my knapsack at the lookout, chose a sector that seemed to have the least concentration of troops, picked out trails leading in that direction, and set off to find it on foot. The sun was coming up over the eastern mountains by the time I crossed the river and neared the edge of the camp. Campfires that had warmed them at night had gone out: new ones were being built to cook the morning meal. Only the sleepy guards and the cooks were up and about. I picked out a particularly sleepy-looking guard who was slouched against a tree. The makeshift sign just in front of his post announced: HQ-Zed Compania—Headquarters of Z Company.

"Atención," the guard said as I approached. He came to attention himself, more or less.

I put on my most sheepish grin, honed up a slurred, drunken Spanish, and told the guard that I was Sgt. Luis Pequeno of B Company, returning from a marvelous night with a local talent on one of the peasant farms. I said I was trying to get to my home company before reveille and would appreciate it if he didn't make a fuss and get me in difficulty with my lieutenant.

He grinned back his understanding and passed me on without missing a yawn. I was in.

I found B Company's headquarters' sign two hundred yards farther up the valley, adroitly circumvented it by crossing a high slope, and came into the purview of J Company up near the entrance to the main trail to the mountain, to Alto Arete. I loitered in the area for some time, taking in the terrain and the probable intelligence and alertness of the guards at the gate there, then was circling back to the area of Z Company where I hoped to forage for food. The smell of cooking up and down the narrow hollow was wrinkling my stomach and making me drool. It occurred to me that I hadn't eaten since noon yesterday. I had been busy during the dinner hour keeping watch over my quarry, Sergeant Pequeno, whom I had followed from that canteen in the capital to the home of Jorge and Melina Cortez—and to Elicia.

I stepped brazenly up to the three wiry cooks who were working at a primitive table, chopping up chicken and vegetables and tossing them helter skelter into a huge black pot over a blazing fire. With a few well-chosen lies, some sly winks and comments about the drawing power of the local lasses, I managed to cadge food. The first lie concerned my alleged special mission from Colonel Vasco. The cooks were mightily impressed with my status, so I ate well, crouched against a tree where I kept a wary eye out for scorpions. I should have been keeping a wary eye on the cooks; one of them disappeared while I dined on the stew and I never even noticed that he was gone.

"Atención!" It was a sharp command, sharply given. I looked up into the face of a man who had obviously done brutal things in his approximately forty five years of existence on earth. He was tall and broad, with an immense shock of black hair that was giving over grudgingly to gray. His broad chest was bedecked with enough medals to give an ordinary man fatigue just from carrying them around. "*Su nombre y jefe, por favor.*"

I stood and, even though I'm a tall man well over six feet, I found myself looking up at the rough, scarred, pockmarked face of the officer. From his insignia, I guessed him to be Colonel Ramon Vasco. And he had demanded my name and the name of my commander.

"Sergeant Luis Pequeno," I responded swiftly, standing at attention. "My commander, Captain Rodrigues, has sent me from the guerilla encampment to warn that an American may have infiltrated his encampment."

The colonel studied me for a moment, trying to satisfy himself if I were an imposter, or merely stupid. I had tried to convey the idea of stupidity, had obviously succeeded. The thinnest part of my story concerned Captain Rodriguez. I knew no such man and was only guessing that, in a detachment of a thousand Cuban Marines, there had to be a captain named Rodrigues.

"What is Rodrigues doing with the guerillas?" the colonel asked. "He belongs with Q Company, right down the mountain there."

"He was sent with a few of us to investigate some unrest among the conscripted peasants," I said quickly, counting on the story about Antonio to be a common one.

"I have no memory of authorizing such a change in the captain's assignment." The colonel was still studying me, still convinced that he was witnessing stupidity, but perhaps also seeking a rat in disguise.

"I believe it was your adjutant who authorized the change," I said. I wasn't even sure the colonel had an adjutant.

"All right," he said finally. "Tell Captain Rodrigues that his message has been delivered. We know there's an American on the island, but he was last seen in the capital. There's no possibility of him showing up here—and certainly he will never find the guerilla encampment. Get back to your post now."

I moved away, swiftly, wanting to put a lot of distance between me and the strong, surly and obviously vicious colonel.

"Atención, Pequeno!" the colonel snarled.

I was torn between standing at attention and running like a castrated wildcat.

"Not that way, stupido," Colonel Vasco said, laughing at my now obvious stupidity. "That way lies the lower minefield. Go back the way you came, over there."

Thank God, he was pointing off to his right, or I would have taken off in another wrong direction. Thanks to the colonel, though, I was finally on the way to the Guerillas. It could very easily have gone sour, though, gone all wrong. Sometimes, a little stupidity can work miracles.

But the misdirection wasn't what was making me sweat so much as I walked away over the small rise. I was sweating because I had just come through that section which the colonel had said was the lower minefield. The main miracle was that I hadn't stepped in the wrong place and been blown to bits.

Even so, the way to the guerilla encampment wasn't as simple as the colonel had made out. Within two hundred yards up a narrow trail leading from the main hollow, I was hopelessly lost. The trail ended and I stood gazing at walls of jungle. Vines riddled the high trees, creating a network of obstacles. Underbrush added spice to the sealed wall of green.

I was about to turn back, to seek another trail

through, when a section of jungle shook, rattled and then moved aside. A grizzled man in peasant clothes and a Russian rifle slung over his bony shoulder, stepped into the opening and grinned at me.

"Are you lost, sergeant?" he asked in Spanish.

"No," I said, thinking fast. "I've been serving as courier most of the night and was on the trail when today's password was given out. I was afraid I'd be shot if I called out to you."

I knew enough about military operations to know about passwords and the daily changing of them. And I knew that this was a checkpoint where a password would be required.

"How do you know of this place?" the guerilla demanded, eyeing me with even greater suspicion, unslinging his XZ-47. "Only the leaders and a few select guards know of this place."

Obviously, I couldn't tell him that I'd merely stumbled onto it. Well, I had fooled Colonel Vasco with the story about a special assignment from Captain Rodrigues. I would move up in the chain of command.

"I was told of it by Colonel Vasco himself," I said, looking brazenly into the peasant face and keeping a sharp eye also on his hands that clutched the Russian rifle.

"And why did he not give you the password?"

"As I told you," I said, pretending exasperation, "I have been two days on the trail. I was not able to receive today's password."

He looked me over good, checking to see if the uniform really was mine, I supposed. The uniform fit like a glove, but the man still didn't seem impressed or convinced.

"Whom do you seek?"

"On orders from Colonel Vasco," I said, emphasizing the name of the obviously dreaded and feared military leader, "I am to locate a man by the name of Antonio Cortez and to bring him to headquarters."

The guerilla studied me much the way the colonel had studied me, trying to assess the depth of my stupidity, or my shrewdness.

"This Antonio Cortez," he said, slowly, clutching his rifle and walking through the opening of the jungle wall. I peered around him and saw that he was alone, that the thick vines and underbrush he had so easily moved rode on a wooden platform with huge rubber tires. It was an effective and ingenious camouflage. "Who is he and why is he so important to the colonel?"

I shrugged and looked as stupid as I could manage. "I am but a courier. I don't involve myself with the reasons behind the commands of my betters."

The guerilla laughed, coughed and spat up a wad of phlegm. The wad landed on my right boot. As I was studying the situation down there, trying to decide if he had done that on purpose, the guerilla swung his rifle and caught me in the forehead with the butt. I went down, my eyes watering from the blow, but still painfully conscious.

"You stupid fool," the guerilla said, shifting the rifle around and jamming the muzzle into my throat. "If you had come from Colonel Vasco, you would know the password. He gives it to the couriers the night before the change. Sometimes, they have a week of passwords in their knowledge, just in case they are on the trail when the regular troops are given the daily change. And, if you were from the colonel, you would know that Antonio Cortez is in the stockade, scheduled to be shot at noon today, along with twenty two other trouble-makers and would-be deserters." He pressed harder with the gun barrel, almost cutting off my wind. "Who are you and what do you want here? Be quick and be truthful, my friend, or you will never be anything else but food for the maggots, scorpions and ants in this jungle."

I was about to ask why he would cheat the pigs out of a good meal, but decided flipness wasn't called for just now. Besides, he hadn't yet guessed that I was an American. That was good—or was it? Perhaps the truth would give me a few more minutes of life. There was no way I could reach and use Wilhelmina, Hugo or Pierre before this man pulled the trigger of his automatic rifle and reduced me to an entree for insects.

"I am the American everyone seeks," I said, corrupting my Spanish a bit to convince him of my gringo status. "I want to be taken to Colonel Vasco. I have important information for him, about an American attack being planned."

His eyes widened, but he didn't ease back on the rifle barrel. It was still jammed into my windpipe. I had spoken those words in a kind of falsetto, gasping for enough air to breathe, much less to talk. His eyes narrowed again and the grin was back.

"My instructions are to. . ."

"I know your instructions," I said, gasping out the words. "Disembowel all Americans and feed them to the pigs. But I have important news for the colonel. You'll be in great trouble if the news doesn't reach him in time."

He eased back on the rifle, but didn't lower his guard. "Why were you coming this way when the colonel is in the opposite direction? And what is this business about taking Antonio Cortez to see Colonel Vasco?"

I knew I couldn't do Antonio any more damage, especially since he was to be shot at noon. I would involve him more deeply in my web of truth and lies.

"Antonio Cortez is one of the key contacts for the Americans being sent to Nicarxa," I said, moving away from the rifle and sitting up on the ground.

The rifle moved back to my neck, forcing me to lie supine again. The guerilla's scowl was back.

"Cortez is just a boy," he said, sneering. "What could he know of Americans, of being an important contact. He is nothing, a peasant lad who fell into the wrong company and got himself a death sentence for his opposition to the great Don Carlos."

"Zapata was only nineteen when he set out to destroy the tyrannical rulers of Mexico," I said, drawing on my knowledge of revolutionaries.

"And he was killed for his efforts."

"But only after great successes in the field."

"True. All right. Stand up. Do it carefully. I will take you to my chief and let him decide what to do about you."

As I stood, I pressed the trigger release on Hugo and the stiletto slid easily into my hand. But the guerilla kept his rifle aimed at my throat and I had no chance to charge him. We moved through the fake opening in the jungle wall. Once that opening was closed, I knew my goose would be cooked.

This man's chief, I knew, would radio Colonel Vasco and, when the two compared notes, the colonel would know that I was the man who had fooled him. In his ire, he might well order me shot, disemboweled and fed to anyone or anything that happened to be hungry.

The bearded guerilla lowered the rifle and reached for a handle to roll the intricate gate back into place. It was my moment. I stepped in close, knocked the rifle aside and, before the man could call out, I rammed Hugo into his throat, twisted, gouged and pulled sharply upward. He died instantly and my remorse was minimal.

I pushed the opening aside again, dragged the guerilla's body through and back down the trail. I pressed my way into the jungle wall beside the trail, dropped the dead body in a thicket and arranged the undergrowth so that it didn't look as though it had been disturbed in a hundred years. It would take them days to find him, and then only by following their noses.

Once inside the compound, though, with the camouflaged gate back in place, I had no idea where to go, no idea how many more guerillas were between me and the stockade where Antonio was awaiting execution. Once again, I would have to follow my own nose and hope that it didn't lead me through minefields or up against men like Colonel Vasco.

It took only a half hour to find the stockade. Suspicion seemed to drop away from the guerillas now that I was inside the compound. It was inconceivable to them that any unauthorized person could make it this far; and the Cuban uniform kept them in awe. They were afraid to challenge the Cuban Marine sergeant who walked with a purposeful step and seemed to know precisely where he was going and what he was doing. Little did they know that I was a babe in the wilderness. A dangerous babe, but a babe nonetheless.

The stockade was recognizable by its high, barbed-wired fence, the armed guards around its makeshift gate and the scraggly, woebegone unarmed peasants peering out through the fence. I strode up to the guards and was pleasantly surprised when they snapped to attention. It was a plus gained for me by the arrogant Cubans and I decided to make best use of that plus.

"Bring the prisoner Antonio Cortez to the gate," I ordered in my best Cuban Spanish. "He is to be interrogated regarding information he may possess about an American who has come to Nicarxa to interfere with the revolution."

The guards—four of them—stared at me and at each other. They didn't seem about to follow the order with any degree of expeditiousness.

"Hurry it up, damn you," I said, being as arrogant as I knew the Cubans to be with these simple peasants. "Colonel Vasco is waiting for this information. Bring Cortez out here."

They bumped about a lot, into each other and even into the barbed wire where they snagged their already tattered clothes. But they got the gate open and, while three of them poised with aimed rifles at the motley crew of prisoners behind the fence, one of them went in to fetch a skinny, dark-haired, black-eyed boy who looked enough like Elicia to have been a twin. The build was different, though, and the height.

Antonio Cortez looked surly and uncooperative as the guard brought him to me. He seemed about to spit on my boots and I wouldn't have blamed him. If he had, though, I would have had to knock him flat for his efforts, to keep up my image as a Cuban non-com.

"Come with me," I said, palming Sergeant Pequeno's forty five and leveling it at Antonio. I glanced over my shoulder at the guards. "It's all right," I said. "I must interview him out of earshot. I will take full responsibility."

They seemed nervous about it, but the one man closed the gate again and the others lowered their rifles and snapped again to attention. It was working like a charm. So far.

When we were out of earshot, I turned to face Antonio, my back to the guards so that they couldn't read my lips if they were so inclined. That was a mistake on my part, but I didn't know it then.

"Don't say anything, Antonio," I said. "And don't express any surprise at what I have to say. Just listen and keep looking surly and angry. Do you understand?"

"Who are you?"

"A friend. An American. I was sent here by your sister." His eyes widened and a smile flickered on his lips. "Don't change expressions," I snapped. "Damn it, the guards are watching." The surly look came back.

"How do I know you speak the truth?"

"For one thing," I said, losing patience, "You have no choice. You're to be shot in a few hours. If I work it right, I may be able to walk out of here with you, pretending that I'm taking you to Colonel Vasco."

"Sure," he said, really surly now. "And once we're out of the compound, you'll kill me yourself."

"Don't be stupid. If I wanted you dead, I could fire right now. Better still, I could leave you for your little party at noon. There's another thing." I fished the gold chain and locket from my pocket. "Your sister gave this to me. There's a note folded up in the locket. You can't take a chance on reading it now. You have to trust me. And we. . ."

"You bastard," Antonio exploded. "You took this from her. You killed her and took this and came trying to convince me to tell what I know of the counter-revolution."

"Again," I said, sighing more deeply as patience ran thin, "don't be stupid. I left Elicia very much alive at the home of your cousin. She gave me that chain and. . ."

"What is our cousin's name?"

I told him the name Elicia had given me, having never met the cousin.

"You could have gotten the name from the authorities," he snapped. "They know all my family and will kill them as soon as I'm executed. But of course you know all that since you are from the authorities."

"And you're strictly from hunger," I said, losing all patience with this bullheaded little counter-revolutionary. "Listen to me. I'll tell you how I happen to be here."

I told him about following the Cuban Marine, about stopping him from raping Elicia. I made the mistake then of telling him that it was one of a series of rapes. He exploded in rage before I finished.

"You filthy pigs," he screamed. I could hear— even feel—the guards stirring behind me. At any moment, they would open fire on Antonio, kill him and then bring the local commander to question me about what the hell was going on. I held up a hand to shush the hothead, but he was off on a tirade.

"I will kill you all for what you've done to my sister. I will not die at noon, you filthy bastard. I will live and I will lead the counter-revolutionaries to wipe every stain of you from the face of Nicarxa. You come to me with a chain and a locket that you took from my sister while you were defiling her, you fucking animal. . ."

The guards were rushing up behind me now. I could hear the click and slap of their rifles as cartridges were injected into the chambers. I had only seconds to act, and it would take a week to calm down the raging Antonio Cortez.

I leaped forward and knocked the slender Nicarxan flat on his ass. In the same motion, I had Wilhelmina in my left hand. I whirled as the startled guards tried to decide where they should aim their rifles—at me or at the fallen Antonio.

They hesitated too long. I let fly with both guns —Wilhelmina and the Marine sergeant's sidearm forty five. With four well-aimed shots, I downed all four guards.

But there was a hue and cry all around the camp beyond the stockade and I saw fresh guards gathering up weapons and running in our direction. I reached down and grasped Antonio's hand, pulling him to his feet.

"Follow me," I snapped. "If you do, we might have a chance of getting out of here. If you don't, then you can go to hell for all I care."

I took off running, hoping I hadn't lost my sense of direction for the trail that had brought me into this nest of trouble.

CHAPTER THREE

There was no way I could use the gas bomb, even if I could get to it in time. I would have killed Antonio's friends in the stockade—and there were more of them than I first thought. The sound of the shots brought dozens of them out of low, mean huts into the stockade yard.

And guerillas and Cuban Marines were streaming out of barracks beyond the stockade. Running alone wouldn't do it for us. I had to create a diversion.

"Get the guards' rifles, and sidearms," I shouted to Antonio as I sprinted for the gate in the barbed wire fence. "Come on. Make it quick."

I opened the gate and the dissident guerillas came streaming out, going for the weapons that Antonio was already assembling in a pile. Antonio himself clutched a Russian automatic Volska and was priming the chamber for an assault on the on-rushing guards.

We both opened fire at the same time, Antonio

with the wicked Volska, me with Wilhelmina and
the forty five. The guerillas all hit the dirt, flat on
their bellies. Some of them even turned and ran.
But the Cuban Marines, better trained and better
motivated, kept on coming.

Just when it looked as Antonio and I would be
overwhelmed by the Marines, who had already
opened fire on the run, a half-dozen of Antonio's
friends took professional stances to our right and
opened a withering fire against approaching
Marines. Their three Volskas and three forty fives
thundered in the dusty compound.

This time, even the Cubans took cover. There is
such a thing as bravery and dedication: there is also
such a thing as stupidity. The Cubans weren't stupid.

In that brief respite, while the Marines were
seeking cover—and while some of them were
shouting at the other guerillas to come out of hiding—I tugged Antonio's sleeve and nodded toward
the narrow trail leading back into the jungle.
Hopefully, it was the one leading to the camouflaged gate on wheels.

"We'll retreat in alternate waves," I said. "Let's
take a point at the trail's entrance, then open fire
while your friends fall back."

It worked like a charm. Or almost like one. It
was aided by Antonio's unarmed friends who had
been dashing around in the compound, creating
confusion by looking for weapons. Some of them
were brave enough to dash all the way to the first
group of fallen Cubans to rob them of weapons.

Antonio and I, along with two of his rebel
friends, took up positions at the entrance to the
trail. We opened fire again on the regrouped

Cubans, careful to miss Antonio's scrambling, hus-
tling friends. As we fired, more than a dozen of the
rebels dashed past us up the trail, found a high
point on the hillside and began firing down on the
Cubans.

"Okay. Our turn next. Let's get on the trail."

"No," Antonio said sharply. "I stay here until
they're all dead."

He was one hard head. "Look, champ," I said,
"if you don't move your ass right now, I'm going
to pump a bullet into it. There's no time for arguments. Colonel Vasco's whole damned batallion
will be here in a matter of minutes. Now move it."

To emphasize my command, I held the forty five
aimed at his head. That surly look came back and
he considered resisting even me. But he fired another burst from the Volska, sent a squad of
Cubans flying into the dirt, and then hot-footed it
up the trail. I went after him.

We reached the high point and I waved the rebels on. Three more had joined us and we took the
high point to protect the trail's entrance. Unfortunately, we all ran out of bullets just as a huge
gang of Cubans and Nicarxan guerillas reached the
point we were trying to protect.

That's when I used Pierre. The little gas bomb
sailed above the jungle and lit just in front of the
running troops. They began instantly to gag as the
pale blue cloud exploded around them. Antonio
looked at me, incredulous, then a smile came to
erase the surliness.

"Excellent work. You're killing them all."

"Not all," I said. "And if we don't move out of
here, that gas will catch up to us on the wind. Let's
go—and no arguments this time."

"I am with you," he said.

The five of us ran single file up the trail. It was so narrow that we could have defended it against an army if only we had enough ammunition. At the top of the trail, where the false wall was in place, the other dissidents had stopped, believing themselves to be hemmed in. There was a rumbling of anger as I came into the small clearing. I was the one they thought had led them into a trap.

I put on my best smile and held up my hands.

"Don't be alarmed, gentlemen," I said. "There's a way out. Unfortunately the leaders also know it, so we haven't much time. Listen closely."

I told them they were the nucleus of a counter-revolutionary group to overthrow Don Carlos, kick out the Cubans and make the necessary peace with the Apalcans. I established the high ledge above the valley floor overlooking the main Cuban contingent as our meeting place and soon-to-be command post. Most of them knew where it was.

"All right. As soon as we leave this compound, I want you to fan out on all the trails. Travel in twos. Find weapons and ammunition when and where you can. If you kill, don't let it be a waste. Take the time to search the man you kill. Take all his weapons. We'll meet on the ledge in six hours. That will be at 3 P. M."

They all nodded agreement and then gaped with astonishment as I pulled the huge rolling hunk of jungle from its nest. Laughing and grinning, they began to file through.

Right into the teeth of vicious gunfire.

Colonel Vasco's men had arrived and had sealed off this exit. Antonio's friends were dropping like flies. I felt a sickness seeing the massacre and knowing that I'd caused it, knowing that I was *in* it.

I nearly panicked then, considering it all lost. But I spotted two full ammo belts dropped by one of Antonio's friends. I snatched them up and grabbed Antonio's arm.

"This way. Back down the trail."

He started to resist, knowing that a return to the compound was probably suicide. But going ahead was certain suicide. He came along, snatching up an extra Volska as we ran.

Everything wasn't lost, though. I had learned one important lesson in traveling jungle trails with their unrelenting walls. The lesson was that jungle walls aren't all that unrelenting. Even the thickest walls of foliage have weak points, but it takes a trained and observant eye to spot those weak spots. On the way up the trail, I had spotted at least two areas where a man could push through and cover himself from behind.

I led Antonio to the nearest, we pushed through and crouched in the dim bower of leaves and vines. We'd no sooner settled on the damp, dark ground when footsteps came thundering past from below. Pierre had done his stuff, but there is a limit as to how long a gas bomb can remain effective. The trail was clear of gas below and the Cubans and guerillas were coming.

We waited, fearful of making a move or a sound. And then came voices, muffled and mumbling at first, then louder and closer. Along with the voices came the thrashing sounds of machetes hacking at the walls of the trail.

"He's still in the compound," came the shrill, angry voice of Colonel Ramon Vasco. "The fucking gringo has outsmarted all of you. Well, by

God, you find him or you will all live to regret it. *I want that man.* Do you hear me?"

Christ, I thought, the whole Caribbean can hear you. I looked around to see if there were a way out of this cul de sac. There wasn't, unless we did a little of our own hacking. But we had no machetes and the noise would have pinpointed our hiding place.

I hadn't outsmarted the colonel's guerillas and Marines. I had outsmarted myself.

The colonel was still belching out orders, telling how he would personally find out the purpose of my mission before performing the indelicate surgical technique known among brutes as disembowelment, evisceration. The machetes were still hacking at the walls of the jungle on either side of the narrow trail, drawing closer to our niche.

I heard a scratching and scraping nearby and saw that Antonio was using his Volska rifle to work at the soft ground behind us.

"Que pasa?" I whispered. "What are you doing?"

"The soil is soft and most roots are not as strong as that which grows above the ground. We can dig our way through the roots."

At first, I thought he'd lost his mind. It would take hours, even days, to go more than a few yards in this thick jungle. Even as I was thinking that, Antonio lifted a huge clump of roots and soil and edged himself past it. He worked almost silently. What small scraping sounds he did make were covered by the shouts of the colonel, the hacking of the machetes and the grunting of the men weilding them.

I put my own rifle to work on a clump of bushes

just ahead of Antonio. The dirt came away so easily that we might have been two kids on the beach, scooping out sand to bury the beach bully.

By the time the machetes were alongside our niche, we had progressed twenty feet into the jungle, replacing each bush we had dug up. There was virtually no sign of us having passed through. Or so we hoped.

"Ah, I thought I had found them," we heard a Cuban say, "but it's merely a small opening that leads nowhere."

"Don't dawdle," the colonel belched. "If they aren't there, move on down and find another opening. Find him. Find the fucking gringo."

We were safe. We were also exhausted, hungry, thirsty and very much in need of biological relief. We had worked ourselves into a place so small and tight with vines that we couldn't have worked a sneeze into our regimen without getting a hernia. So we lay there, gazing up through the thick foliage, watching tiny fingers of sunlight try to penetrate the gloom.

In a few minutes, the jungle was quiet, except for a muffled hacking down below. In an hour, there was no sound but the birds that had returned after the passing of the Cubans and the guerillas and the gas. Antonio was preparing to start working his way back to the trail, but I had a hunch that our enemies hadn't finished with the trail.

"Wait."

"For what? They are gone. They search for us elsewhere, and I have to move or I will die right here."

"You won't die unless you do move," I said. "Just wait."

Within minutes, we heard them on the trail

again. They weren't looking for us now. They had come back to carry down the dead men, Antonio's friends who had been massacred when I opened up that damned gate.

"I must learn to listen to you, Senor," Antonio said, a ring of genuine gratefulness in his voice.

"You'd better learn something," I said, smiling at him, "or that hot head of yours will get you killed."

"It almost did," he said. "I spoke out too soon, before my friends were prepared to act. I was responsible for getting us all locked up in the compound and sentenced to die at noon today."

Somehow, I wasn't surprised. But I dropped the issue then. I fished out the chain and locket again and told him to read the note from Elicia. He did, straining in the dim light to make out the words. When he had read it, his face was part smile, part concern.

"I must thank you for saving her from that cruel fate," he said. "She is safe now, but what about my parents?"

"They refused to leave the farm. But I don't think the Cubans will bother them—they're so old and helpless, and they're blameless."

His face was a wicked scowl.

"You don't know these bastard Cubans," he said. "Their plans are long-ranging. When Don Carlos is in control, the Cubans will come in droves. They will be looking for land. Shrewd Cuban commanders are already having our old citizens killed and legally taking over their land. When others come, they will receive high prices for land taken by blood. They have every reason to kill my parents."

"And we have every reason to stop them, starting with Don Carlos."

"You make the commands," he said, smiling openly now, "and I will obey. Without question."

The boy had grown up very fast, the hard way.

But I waited another hour before we slipped out of our hiding place. We did it carefully, replacing each bush and vine we had uprooted. We had no reason to conceal the hiding place now, but I wanted that vicious colonel to think we'd slipped through his fingers by some kind of magic, or genius. I wanted him to over-estimate my powers. An enemy that over-estimates is just as vulnerable as one that under-estimates.

Three hours later, at noon, the time Antonio and his friends had been slated for execution, we were on the small ledge far below his parents' farm, where I had hidden my radio. I cranked up the batteries and tuned to the special frequency used by all AXE agents to make secret contacts from the field. As N3, the top Killmaster for AXE, a call on that frequency would clear the boards at the AXE office on DuPont Circle in Washington.

David Hawk, my boss, had never failed me. If a call came from me from the middle of the Pacific, there would be planes and/or nuclear submarines to my rescue within minutes. Once, Hawk had even commandeered a Navy aircraft carrier and all its planes to pluck me out of danger.

When I got the AXE office in Washington, I gave the coded response and asked for a direct link to David Hawk.

"Unavailable," came the terse response. "What is your message, N3?"

I tried to hide the disappointment in my voice as

I described the hopelessness of assaulting Mount Toro and Alto Arete. I provided details given to me by Luis Pequeno (and confimed by Antonio Cortez) about the thousand Marines, the backup guerillas, the broken trails, the fact that the sides of the mountain were seeded with poison-laden bits of metal. I told of Don Carlos Italla's plans for an all-out war in six days. I told of the anti-aircraft batteries operated by computers, of the minefields at the top and bottom of the mountain, of the electrified fence and the rabid guard dogs and armed monks. I told of Antonio's small group of dissidents, a few of whom had apparently escaped the ambush, and of others Antonio knew about and with whom we hoped to make contact. I told of the group coming from Apalca to meet with Don Carlos to plan Apalcan support for his revolution. Finally, I told of how Don Carlos would annihilate the peace commission trying to work out a treaty between Nicarxa and Apalca.

"And what is it you want from AXE?" the anonymous voice responded.

The way he asked the question made my insides quiver. His tone implied that no matter what I asked I wouldn't get it.

"The least I need is an airdrop of food, weapons and ammunition in a place I will designate," I said. "What I'd really like is a small detachment of Blue Light Commandos to help me neutralize. . ."

"One moment, please, N3," the curt voice said.

He was gone for a hell of a long time and I was beginning to understand Antonio's hotheadedness, his lack of patience. I wanted to fling the damned radio off the mountain.

"Special message from the President," the voice came back on. "There is to be no further involvement by this country. No airdrop. No detachment of commandos. You're to accomplish this mission on your own, N3, with no connection whatsoever with your country of origin."

"Dammit, man," I snapped, "my cover is already blown. They know I'm an American and they know I'm here to stop Don Carlos. They know. . ."

"Your problems to solve," the radio voice said. "You and you alone. Over and out, N3. Please do not contact us again on this frequency until your mission is completed and you wish to make your final report."

The radio went dead, the connection broken. I almost did throw the thing off the mountain, but Antonio was watching me closely for my reaction. I smiled, in spite of myself. So much for Hawk's readiness to pluck me out of trouble no matter where I was or how deep the trouble.

"You heard the man, Antonio. We're on our own."

He was about to say something when we heard the twig snap behind us. We had already loaded up the two Russian Volskas with the extra clips, but had thrown away the empty forty fives. They were too heavy to carry around, waiting to find extra clips. I had taped Wilhelmina to the small of my back, where she usually rested. I had stashed extra 9mm cartridges with the radio, but hadn't yet reloaded the luger.

Antonio was the first to respond. He flopped to his stomach and poked the bulky Volska out ahead of him, aiming at the direction of the noise of the breaking twig. I shuttled the radio back into its niche between three rocks, snatched up and pocketed two extra clips for Wilhelmina, then went to the firing position.

We waited perhaps three minutes, listening to silence from the forest behind our secure ledge. Birds called. Wind whistled up from the lovely Reina Valley. There was, however, no sign of human or animal presence near us. Antonio was about to rise again when we heard the snapping again. Then came several snappings. Christ, there must be a whole battalion out there. How had they found us?

The drop from the far end of the ledge was more than twenty feet, with no slant. At the bottom was a bare area of gravel and sharp rocks, then the thick jungle below that. Even if we made it over the side without breaking any bones—more specifically, our necks—we'd have a few dozen feet of open terrain to cross before reaching the cover of the jungle.

We had no choice. The hill behind us was filling up with Marines or guerillas, or both, getting into position to catch us in a crossfire that not even the ants would escape with their antennae intact.

Although I was convinced that they could see us, or had seen us earlier and were moving up by quadrant positions, I sensed another opportunity to build my image as a magician with the good Colonel Vasco. I motioned for Antonio to follow me.

Using my elbows as legs, I edged across the narrow ledge to one side, where the drop to the rocky area below wasn't quite so high or so steep. We eased over the edge like a couple of eels. We were no sooner dropping through space than I heard the sharp bark of the colonel.

"Fire, fire fire! Annihilate them!"

He had obviously lost his desire to quiz me and then personally remove my intestines. He wasn't about to let me slip away again as he had back there on the compound trail.

Antonio and I hit the ground at the same time. He landed lightly, flipping over in the air to keep his feet. I miscued slightly and came down on an angle, pitching forward and clanking my ankle on an outcropping of rock. The pain rumbled up through my body like a tidal wave of pellets. I stifled a yell, unwilling to give the colonel even a brief moment of pleasure.

We were off and running—me limping—even before the Marines and guerillas stopped firing. We were in the dark trees before they appeared on the ledge above. I knew they would expect us to run straight down the steep hill through the trees.

"You go left," I said to Antonio, gasping from the pain that was still running its course through my bones. "I'll go right. Stay near the top of the hill. When you're clear, meet me at the lookout point I told about, the one overlooking the valley and Mount Toro."

Further instructions were cut off by a fusillade of bullets tearing through the trees. Antonio took off, as directed. I ran-limped the other way, hearing the shots above me and the bullets thudding into the rocky soil right behind me.

I hadn't gone twenty feet when the bullet caught me. It was a ricochet off a rock, but it was just as effective as if it had come straight from the muzzle of the Russian automatic weapon. I felt the dull thud in the soft part of my left side, toward the back. I kept running, though, waiting for a hail of bullets to cut me down.

I made it three hundred yards before I collapsed from the pain. My ankle throbbed like a tympanny drum. My side, bleeding profusely now, felt as though a shark had taken a bite out of it. Weakness came with the pain and I had to rest.

There were no further gunshots from above. Soon, though, I heard them thrashing down through the trees. Most of the search party was heading downhill, but the colonel, wising up to me now, had sent some of his men on sideways sorties. It wouldn't take too many of them to finish me off.

I got, up, ignoring the pain and weakness as much as was humanly possible—which wasn't much—and stumbled along for another two hundred yards, then started straight downhill. I was giving them a hell of a lot of jungle to search. I just hoped I didn't get lost in the process.

Within an hour, I was lost, and didn't care. The pain was a steady rasping throughout all of me, no longer concentrated in my ankle and side. Weakness was also constant, and building with galloping speed. I could tell that my mind was flirting with delerium and I tried to keep clear thoughts, make clear decisions.

But one trail looked like another. All streams seemed to be the same stream that I had already crossed, and re-crossed. All rocks in my path seemed like rocks I had fallen over miles back. I went on and on, up and down the hill. Sometimes, I rambled over high ranges where the trees were sparse and the going easy. Sometimes, I plunged down steep ravines and found myself in thick jungle where the going was all but impossible.

I kept on, knowing that it was necessary to lose myself in order to lose the enemy. I knew also that I had to stop the bleeding in my side or I would simply phase myself out in that thick jungle. I stopped at a stream beside a mossy bank. I took off my shirt, with painful exactitude, and looked at the wound. It was ragged. The bullet must have been in the process of breaking up when it struck me. There were at least three punctures, one large and two small. Blood was streaming from each of them.

I tore off a piece of my shirttail, having the presence of mind to make a small mental pun about tearing off a piece of tail, and gathered up some wet moss. I wrapped the moss in the fragment of shirt material and, using the tape that had held Wilhelmina in place, I stuck the soggy bandage against the wound and taped it into place.

New pain shot through me, threatening to black me out. I took deep breaths and remember thinking how nice it would be to crawl inside that mossy bank and to go to sleep, only to awaken as a carefree and unhunted insect or worm. What sweet bliss that would be.

Strangely, the memory of Elicia's farewell kiss was what brought a sense of reality to my mind. I remembered that dark night on the dirt road near her cousin's hut when she had stood on tiptoe to kiss me, sweetly, firmly. I hadn't been kissed in so innocent and pleasant a fashion since I was a teenager in high school. Perhaps my fond recollection of that kiss had something to do with the fact that Elicia, if she were in the United States, would be a relatively carefree teenager in high school. Instead, she was a peasant girl on this tormented island, open prey to the two-legged animals from another island, destined to grow old, abused, wornout and desolate by the time her teen years had barely gone by. My God, I thought, we Americans really have it soft.

And then I mentally crossed out the "we." At the moment, I was one American who didn't qualify for the soft life.

I moved on then, and the pain strangely abated in my side. My ankle continued to make its presence known, though, so the going was still difficult. By mid-afternoon, I had just about had it. My thoughts were weird and detached and I knew that I was getting delerious by leaps and bounds.

I saw myself running naked on a Caribbean beach, pursued by a flock of naked beauties. Even as I was considering turning to face them, and my delicious fate, the image shattered and I was sliding down a mountain of hot lava, feeling my body actually being cooked by the intense heat. I went suddenly cold and aroused to find myself submerged in a cold, fast-running creek. The water was loosening the bandage over my wound and I crawled from the creek to dry myself on leaves and to re-apply the bandage.

Hunger rose again in my stomach with a great rumbling. I couldn't be starving. It had been just over twenty four hours since I had eaten, but I had been burning up a lot of calories in that time. And losing a lot of blood.

After an hour or so resting on the creek bank where I failed to build up energy, as hoped, I struck off up a worn path that led up over a slight rise. It wasn't a steep rise, but climbing it was like trying to scale the south wall of Mount Everest. I reached the top, saw that the path disappeared into a wooded ravine, and decided to go down and see where the path led.

I took two steps, my ankle twisted on a rock and sent a searing pain through all my joints. I felt myself passing out and looked skyward for a point in reality. Nothing was real up there. Clouds floated in an azure sky, but they were no longer real to me. They could have been marshmallows in blue jello for all I knew.

The sky suddenly began to race before my eyes. I didn't know that I was falling until I hit the ground and felt stones scraping my face and hands. I was sliding down into the ravine where, something in my demented mind told me, great nests of jungle snakes waited to devour me after filling me with their painful poison.

I awoke and was on my back. There was no cloud-filled blue sky above me. There was a network of vines, expertly thatched into a roof. Around me were walls of the same jungle material, showing the hand of man. To my left was a door, open, showing a small clearing and then green jungle beyond. It seemed to be dusk out there. Or dawn.

The weakness was still with me, but my mind seemed to be functioning clearly. I couldn't feel any pain in my side or my ankle, yet I didn't feel as though I'd been drugged.

The room formed by the thatched walls and roof was small, as though designed for keeping a man or an animal in captivity. It reminded me of a hut used in an African prison camp in which I once spent a few months before Hawk found me and rescued me. But it wasn't hot in this room, the way it had been in the African version.

I started to sit up, to get my bearings a bit better. Something held me and I realized then that I was tied securely. My hands and arms were outspread and tied to stakes driven into the clay earth. Even my head was tied, with soft vines wrapped around it and attached to a stake somewhere behind me. Beneath my torso was a soft pallet of thatched jungle growth.

Strangely, I felt no fear at being tied up in this small, low-ceilinged hut. It was the drugs that made me feel safe, the same drugs that had taken away my pain. But I didn't know that yet.

In place of fear was the whimsical, almost comical, feeling that I was Gulliver reincarnated, that a jungle version of the Lilliputians had tied me in this small hut. I half expected to see tiny, six-inch Indians tippy-toeing into the hut to laugh at me, to point with triumph at the giant they had captured and tied with their little vines.

My first impulse, then, was to call out, to find out if tiny creatures had really brought me here—and why. I thought better of it, knowing that small creatures like the Lilliputians existed only in literature and in the minds of demented people. Something large and real had done this to me. My last memories had been of scudding down a path into a ravine. Yet, I felt no pain in my face and hands that must have been abraded badly in that fall.

Although natural fear didn't build in me—again because of the drugs—I did have a natural suspicion that no sane man, or no friend, would have brought me to this hut and staked me to the ground. Why I hadn't been killed, I didn't know. My mind began to conjure up all sorts of grisly plans my captor might have for me.

I was once again toying with the idea of calling out, to get to the bottom of this mystery if only to satisfy my curiosity and get the atrocities over with, when a shadow fell across the open door. I heard a scuffling footstep outside.

And then a huge, hulking figure appeared in the doorway. It was so tall that I could see only its legs. The figure knelt, and kept on kneeling. I guessed the man's height at around seven feet.

He was staring at me from the open doorway. The light behind him kept me from seeing his face and clothes clearly. But it was obvious that he was a giant and, in that dim light of dusk (it was growing darker, so I knew it wasn't dawn), I could see his eyes sparkling and shiny.

With a sharp drawing in of my breath, I remembered the description I'd been given of Don Carlos Italla. I could hear old Jorge Cortez's words as though he were in the hut with me:

A giant of seven feet, a mountainous specimen of three hundred pounds, eyes like ingots of burning phosphorus, hands that could shred stainless steel slabs. A fury of a monster with a booming voice like the rumble of thunder.

In that moment I knew that Don Carlos Italla's men had found me in that ravine, had brought me here to this hut and staked me down. They had also drugged me to keep me docile.

I knew this for a fact. But I felt no real fear. My only regret, as I peered back at the giant with the massive hands and red, sparkling eyes, was that I hadn't given in to my earlier urges to buy and operate a truck garden along a quiet highway in Ohio.

Soon, there wouldn't be any quiet highways. And no Nick Carter either.

CHAPTER FOUR

"Good evening, Don Carlos," I said, trying to sound flip even though my heart was pounding with a renewal of fear. "Are you doing your own surgery these days?"

The giant said nothing. He had something in his right hand, but I couldn't see what it was. Gun? Knife? Scalpel? He began to crawl into the hut, moving slowly toward me. The thing in his hand got scraped along the clay floor.

Even before the giant reached me, I could smell the overpowering odor of him. It was body odor to the Nth Degree, and it filled the small hut to overflowing. Was Don Carlos Italla soap-shy, along with his other talents?

"Eat, my friend," the giant said in excellent Spanish. "Eat and sleep again. Night comes and I do not talk at night."

He said nothing more. The thing in his hand was a bowl. In the bowl were vegetables cooked in a kind of savory broth that was not from an animal.

The giant fed me the gruel with his massive fingers, poking tidbits through my lips. I was too hungry to consider the fact that those hands probably hadn't been washed in a year. And the gruel was excellent. It was also drugged.

In five minutes after eating, I was sound asleep again. When I awoke, sunlight had turned the clearing outside into a bright, shiny avenue. I could even make out flies and spiders on the walls and ceiling of the low hut.

And the giant came again to kneel in the doorway and peer at me.

It was not Don Carlos. I could see his face more clearly now and it was an old face, full of wrinkles, with a scraggly, undernourished beard. His eyes, though, seemed young and sparkled like agates. He also was not as big as I had thought last night. His bulk came mainly from several layers of coarse clothing that looked as though he might have woven the fabric himself.

"Who are you?" I asked.

"The question, Senor, is who are you? I found you on the trail, lying with your head in a bush and your body burning up with fever. I found nothing on you to say who you are."

"Well, I'm hardly someone to be staked out like an animal," I said, jangling the vine ropes that still held my arms, legs and head.

"There is no law," he said, "that says only the good and the friendly can be wounded and lost in the jungle. You could be one from the mountain. Your wound could have come from one of his enemies. Until I know who you are, you remain tied, as you say, like an animal."

I began to breathe easier then. He was obviously

referring to Alto Arete and Don Carlos. Just as obviously, he was an enemy of Don Carlos. Even more obvious, he was a highly educated and articulate man. His Spanish was of the academic class.

I saw no reason to lie to this man. I told him who I was and described my mission to him. I told him about the Cortez family and how I had saved Elicia and Antonio, only to see Antonio's friends killed in an ambush while following my directions. The old man listened patiently, fixing his attention on each word, regarding me with those glowing eyes. The glow, however, seemed to become warmer as I talked. When I was finished, he remained in his crouch just inside the doorway. I hardly noticed the odor of his body now; I was becoming accustomed to it.

"So I am not an enemy," I continued. "I need your help. The people of Nicarxa need your help. We have only six days to stop Don Carlos from virtually setting the country on fire."

"Four days," he said. "You have slept for two days."

"I was afraid of that," I said. "Why did you drug me?"

He smiled through his wrinkles. "For the healing," he said. "I made a poultice of herbs for your wound, but you were thrashing about in your fever. You would have offset the good of the herbs. I gave you peyote to make your muscles calm themselves."

I didn't ask him how he got the peyote into me when I was unconscious. I had seen Indians in other jungles use primitive bamboo needles to inject themselves with medicines and drugs. I didn't even

want to think of the contraption this man might
have used to inject peyote into my veins.

"All right," I said, gazing from him to the vines
tied to my wrists. "Will you help me? Do you trust
me? Do you know that I'm a friend and not an
enemy?"

"I will help by keeping you tied for yet another
day. If you move now, you will open the wound.
Next time, you might die on the trail."

I was starting to feel panicky. Two precious days
had already slipped by. I had only four days to
reach Alto Arete and stop Don Carlos. I needed
time to organize Antonio and his remaining
friends, enlist more loyal supporters and find a way
through the impregnable defenses of Mount Toro
and Alto Arete.

"I must move around a little," I said, pleading
with the old man, "or my whole body will become
useless. If I promise to stay here with you, to get
my body in shape gradually and leave tomorrow,
will you untie me?"

He considered the request, apparently saw the
logic of it and leaned forward to untie the vines. I
sat up slowly, feeling woozy and weak, fighting the
dizziness that threatened consciousness. I sat there
for a long time, pumping my arms and legs to restore circulation. One more day in that position
and I wouldn't have been able to blink my eyes
without making plans for it first.

Outside the hut, I couldn't open my eyes to the
brightness. I squinted and moved around the clearing, inspecting my new home. We were near the top
of a mountain, on a level plateau. The old man,
whose name was Pico, had come to this place thirty
years ago and had cleared away the trees and brush

to make a home for himself, a home that could not be seen from above or below, and was accessible only by a narrow trail that he took pains to conceal each day with fresh brush.

"I found you," he explained, "when I went to the bottom of my trail to gather bananas, coconuts, mangos and vegetables. Nothing edible grows at this height."

We ate another bowl of gruel and I found in it pieces of coconut and mango. As with last night, it was delicious. As we ate, the old man told his story.

He had been a professor of anthropology at Nicarxa University in his earlier years and had risen to the head of the department of Indian Culture, then had become involved in a plot to unseat a tyrannical leader. For his efforts, he was severely wounded, his family was killed and he was disgraced. He was also unemployed. He fled to the jungle and was captured by the Nincas who lived in the hills not too many miles from this clearing. He lived with the Indians for a time and became friendly with a young warrior who said he detested fighting and wanted to become a monk.

"Our friendship was short-lived," the old man said. "My friend, whose name was Ancio, became more fanatic as the days went by. I heard from others that he and a group of his followers were involved in some kind of sacrificial rites on Mount Toro. No one lived on Alto Arete then. There was no trail to the top of that magnificent column of rock in those days. But Ancio and his followers had found an ancient cave and were using it to make sacrifices to this new gow they had found."

"What were they using as sacrificial victims?" I asked. "Goats? Pigs? Sheep?"

Old Pico's face darkened and he closed his eyes. "The rumors said that they were using children from the Ninca tribe. Their own tribe."

The story didn't shock me because it didn't surprise me. History books are loaded with stories about human sacrifices, most of them children or young girls.

"The story goes that Ancio and his friends would take the children to the cave and burn them there on an altar of stone," Pico went on, opening his eyes and letting them glow like embers at me. "I learned certain truths about this when my own child was taken in the night."

"I thought you said your family was wiped out in the revolution."

He almost smiled. "My first family. When I lived with the Indians, I took a wife and she bore me a daughter. When the daughter was eleven years old, she disappeared. I asked Ancio about her and he said he knew nothing. I could tell by his eyes that he was lying. That was when I followed him and his friends and learned that he had indeed lied, and I came away a broken man. I had heard the rumors about him, about the sacrifices, but I had no proofs." He stopped, unable to go on.

"And you found those proofs," I said.

Ancio's head dropped, like a reluctant nod of assent. "The night I followed Ancio and his friends, they went up Mount Toro, along a difficult trail, and came to a deep place in the ground. I followed them down stone steps into a kind of well that had no water. I remember crawling then through a hole and coming out into a huge cavern deep inside the mountain. What I saw there has all but obliterated my memories of that night."

"What was it you saw there?" I asked. I was sitting forward, my skin tingling as I anticipated the horror of his story.

"It was over," he said. "There was nothing I could do. My daughter had been dead several days, yet they continued to ravage her lifeless body. As I watched, they poured oils over the bodies of several lifeless and ravaged young girls and set the torch. . ."

He stopped, his eyes glowing readily. He closed his eyes. I waited, but there was nothing more to be said. After a brutal death, his eleven-year-old daughter had been sacrificed to Ancio's new and vicious god. She had been burned in that cavern. Ancio raised his head and opened his eyes. He went on, intoning like a ghost:

"My fury was great, perhaps too great. A kind of shock overcame me. I crawled out of that cavern and went up the stone steps of the dry well. I rambled aimlessly on the trail through the whole long night. When daylight came, my fury was still great and so was my shock. It was then that I decided to leave the company of man. Before I left, though, I sought to close up that wicked cavern to prevent further sacrifices, further tortures of the innocent. I sought no revenge against Ancio. His god —or my god—would tend to Ancio's guilt and bring suitable punishment. But I did seek the cavern. I found nothing. In time, I came to this place and built my home. You are the first human I have spoken to in thirty years."

A hermit. A true hermit. I had heard of them and read of them, but I had never met one face to face. I had expected hermits to be silent men, taciturn to a fault, but old Pico seemed willing and ready to talk on and on through the days. And I had only four days to complete a truly impossible mission.

"There is something else in the rumors that you should know," Pico said. "It may not be of help, but you should know of it. It was said that the smoke from the sacrificial fires never came out of the mouth of the cave. It was said that for days after victims were sacrificed, thin plumes of smoke could be seen rising from Alto Arete."

I pondered that for a bit, then knew the answer.

"There's a chimney right up through the middle of the mountain," I said. "A kind of tunnel. There has to be."

"That is what the rumors say. One must not be too trustful of rumors."

But, I was thinking, hating myself for the complicated pun, where there's smoke, there's fire. Where there's smoke, there's also a chimney. A chimney right up through the center of Mount Toro, up through that massive column, and out through the top of Alto Arete.

I spent the day moving slowly about the clearing, even testing my legs on parts of the steep trail down. Most of the time, though, I sat near the hut with Pico and picked the man's brains for more information.

By nightfall, I had learned only that the Ninca tribe still lived in an area near the east slope of Mount Toro, and that Ancio was either their chief or had been killed for his zeal in making human sacrifices. I knew that one of my first moves was to find the Ninca Indians and talk to Ancio if he were still around. If I found that ancient cave, I very well might find a way past Don Carlos Italla's fancy defenses.

That's why I broke my promise to Pico and crept away in the night. I had promised to wait until at least noon and the next day. But my days were slipping away too fast, and I felt strong. I set out for the lookout point, hoping against hope to find Antonio there, alive and well.

Dawn was just starting to break when I neared the lookout point Elicia had shown me the night I took her to her cousin's hut. I would have reached it sooner, but I kept getting lost on Pico's crazy trail.

The wound in my side throbbed with pain, but it hadn't broken open and I was convinced that Pico's work would hold up. Unless, of course, I got into a scrap with a guerilla or a Cuban Marine. Needless to say, my long journey from Pico's hermit hut had been a wary one, avoiding all signs of civilization.

I eased through the foliage, approaching the lookout with caution. Antonio could have been captured and tortured, he could have told the Cubans that he was to meet me here. Then, again Antonio could be hiding there with his rifle at the ready, and could shoot me if I made the slightest noise.

It had always seemed silly to me when I'd read in books that people signalled each other in the night with special bird calls or hooting like owls. It didn't seem silly to me now. I wished that I'd worked out such a plan wih Antonio.

It wasn't necessary. When I slipped into the clearing and scanned the open ledge, Antonio was fast asleep. A friend with him also was asleep. In the dim light of not-quite-dawn, they looked like two logs wrapped in blankets.

Just in case it wasn't Antonio and a friend, I lowered the heavy Russian Volska I'd been carrying and palmed Wilhelmina. I sat to one side of the trail and aimed at the first blanket-covered sleeper.

"Antonio, wake up."

The log raised up, the blanket fell away and there was Elicia Cortez staring down the muzzle of my luger, her eyes wider than saucers.

"Senor Carter," she exploded, much too loudly for comfort. "We thought you were dead."

Antonio stirred in his blanket and I thought perhaps he had also been wounded, worse than me. But he aroused, proving only that he was a sound sleeper.

As I told them all the things that had happened to me since Antonio and I had parted on that steep hillside with bullets raining down from above, Elicia kept watching my every move, hanging on every word. She also kept inching closer, as though I were a campfire and the air was cold.

"We have heard much of the hermit of Mount Toro," Antonio said when I was finished, "but you are the first man to have seen him in thirty years and to tell about it. The stories say that he cooks and eats anyone who comes near his cave."

"The stories are all wet," I said. "For one thing, the man is a vegetarian. He won't kill animals for food or for wearing apparel. For another, he doesn't have a cave—just a hut he built himself out of vines. Now, tell me about yourselves. How did you happen to wind up together? Where are your friends?"

Both faces went gloomy. Elicia stared at the ground, but remained at my side, touching me occasionally with a knee, a hand, an arm. Antonio told how he had found one of his friends, wounded and roaming aimlessly on a trail. The friend had died in his arms. He hadn't found any others.

Finally, he had returned to his parents' house, hoping that perhaps some of his friends had left word there.

"I wish I hadn't gone home," he said sadly. "What I feared would happen has happened. My parents are gone and a bunch of Cuban Marines are living in the house. I asked around, but the neighbors could tell me only that there was shouting and screaming in the night, two days ago. And there was shooting, then silence. I know, Senor Carter, that our parents are dead. Our property now belongs to Colonel Vasco."

And Colonel Vasco, I knew, would sell it at a high price to Cuban immigrants after the bloody revolution put Don Carlos in control and made both Nicarxa and Apalca allies of Cuba. Antonio had reason to be fearful that his parents were dead.

"This may sound ungrateful to the memory of your parents," I said, "but we haven't time to mourn them properly. Our greatest chance is to find the Ninca tribe, get to that sacrificial cave in the mountain and hope to God the chimney is big enough for us to climb up through it."

"I know a shortcut to the Ninca lands," Antonio said, brightening in spite of his grief for his parents. "Are you ready to travel?"

I had traveled all night, but I had also slept and rested for more than two days. I was ready. To make certain, Elicia insisted on carrying my rifle. She would have carried me, if she'd been strong enough. She couldn't seem to show me enough attention, to touch me enough.

It became more and more obvious as we moved along dark trails toward the Ninca lands that Elicia had fallen in love with me. Recalling how I was when I was her age, I wasn't about to under-estimate that love. It was real and it was intense. But I didn't feel the same about her. Ever since my mind had made the connection between Elicia and American high school girls, I had thought of this girl the way a father might feel about a daughter. I had even begun to entertain a fantasy that I might somehow spirit her out of this troubled country and find her a foster home with a friend in the States.

There, I thought in my typically American way of thinking, she could finish out her schooling, live in peace, perhaps fall in love with a handsome blond boy on the football team and settle in sub-urbia with a couple of cars, a dog and mortgage. And, of course, kids.

We were resting beside a clear-running stream along about noontime when Elicia brought me a container of water, sat beside me and gazed up into my eyes. Antonio was off downstream, looking for edible fruits and vegetables.

"I have not thanked you for saving my life," she said.

"I didn't save your life, Elicia," I said, remem-bering that night when the Marine with the enormous organ had tried to rape her. "I merely stopped. . ."

"You saved my life," she said emphatically, placing her slender brown hand on my knee. "I had promised myself that very day that, if the Marines came again and did that to me, I would cut my own throat. What I was living, what I have been living the past three months, has not been life. It has been a kind of horrible death, full of terror and disgust, and no joy. I still feel the disgust."

"For the Marines?"

She looked at me curiously. "No, for myself."

"Why would you be disgusted with yourself? You did nothing wrong?"

She gazed at the ground and took her hand from my knee. "You do not think I am soiled? You do not think I am something for disgust?"

"Good God, no. Why would I think that?"

She didn't respond and I began to think how similar rape victims are the world over. They cannot control what has happened to them, they were unwilling victims of one of man's oldest invasions of privacy, yet they always seemed to feel guilt, or, in the case of Elicia, self-disgust. It was a phenomenon that never ceased to amaze me. I had no words to console the girl, or to change her mind about herself. But I still couldn't remain silent.

"Virginity is important to you, isn't it?" I asked.

Her head snapped up and she looked into my eyes for a time. Then, she looked away and muttered an almost inaudible "yes."

"Then, you must consider yourself a virgin, Elicia. In your mind, you are. You gave nothing of your own free will. It was taken from you. In God's eyes, you are still unspoiled, if that's the way you must look at it."

A fraction of a smile crossed her lips, and then she was sad again. She looked at me, holding my eyes with hers.

"For many months before the Marines came," she said, speaking as though to a priest, in confession, "I had certain thoughts, certain feelings, that I could not control. In spite of all that has happened, I still have those thoughts and those feelings."

I understood perfectly. The girl was a woman, she had thoughts and feelings about sex. She had

had them since she was at least twelve or thirteen. Because she had had them, she felt that what had happened to her was God's will, that she hadn't had her virginity taken from her. She believed her previous thoughts had actually caused the rapes to occur.

"The thoughts and feelings you had and are still having," I said, "are natural thoughts and feelings. Every human and every animal alive has those feelings. They shouldn't be sources of guilt, though. In God's eyes—and in mine—you're still a virgin, still unspoiled, or whatever the word is."

She moved closer, seeming to understand what I was trying to say. Or wanting to understand so badly that she was fooling herself.

"I know what thoughts are natural," she said, "and what thoughts are not. What I am feeling now, for you, is natural. If I am a virgin still, I want you to be the one to receive the fruits of my virginity."

Not even an American high school girl, with all her modern boldness brought on by the national yen for honesty and forthrightness, could have put it more plainly. And very few American high school boys would have turned down such an offer. But I was years away from high school. And I couldn't give as much as I would take.

My silence was my answer. Elicia sat gazing up at me for several seconds, then her eyes fell. I let her think it all out. She would consider all the possibilities. Perhaps I thought of her with disgust, had even lied when I had said that she was still unspoiled, that she had nothing to be ashamed of. Perhaps I thought her beneath me, since I was an obviously important American government agent and she was a lowly Nicarxan peasant girl. Perhaps. . .

"You think me still a child," she said in a low voice, cutting my speculations short. "Well, I am not a child. I have experienced much growing up in the past three months. And yesterday was my birthday. I now am eighteen, legally a woman."

"Happy birthday, Elicia," I said, smiling.

She frowned. "Make with jokes," she said, turning the frown to a womanly look of shrewd knowledge. "All right. Time will pass and you will learn the truth about me, about my womanliness."

She got up without another word and went to help Antonio search for lunch.

When we stopped for our evening break, Antonio and I searched for food while Elicia disappeared into the jungle. She had spent the afternoon trying to impress me with her womanliness. Each time I neared her on the trail, she lowered the bodice of her blouse to expose more of her ample breasts. She bumped against my hips with her wide hips. She carried more and more of our belongings, including all of Antonio's stolen firearms. Now, as we neared exhaustion and she was showing signs of weariness from all the extra effort, she had disappeared.

I found a narrow trail leading down to a grove of banana trees and followed it. I had picked a number of ripe bananas when I heard the splashing just beyond the grove and a wall of vines. I put down the bananas and went to investigate, the Volska rifle slung over my shoulder.

The splashing continued and, when I reached the wall of vines, I heard a low singing. It was Elicia. Her sweet, clear voice rose on the dark jungle air,

singing an old Spanish love song:
"When my love is near me,
I am like the rose,
Budding, billowing, flowering
More than my love knows."

I wondered if she knew that I was near, was listening, perhaps even peeking at her in the stream.
No, I decided. She had no idea that I was near. Her singing was too soft, meant only for her ears. She wasn't putting out a mating call, not yet.

I turned away from the wall of vines, knowing what lovely sight and lovely activities lay beyond it. I had seen this girl in the nude, under extremely vicious circumstances. Seeing her in the nude here, in the stream, and knowing what was going on in her mind and her body, would have spurred me to foolish and damning actions. I may be a killer and an important government agent, but I am no heel. Not on purpose, anyway.

Dinner was a delight. Antonio had found all sorts of fruits and vegetables to add to my bananas. Elicia, however, was the most pleasant of all. She had bathed in the stream and had found orange blossoms to rub against her skin. She smelled good enough to eat, and I had the distinct feeling that she would be better than the fruits and vegetables we were eating. I had trouble keeping my eyes off her, but I decided to merely enjoy the fragrance and the nearness of her, and let it go there.

We rested only two hours after dinner and went on in full darkness. I lost my sense of direction and had no idea which side of Mount Toro we were on. Antonio seemed to know exactly where we were going and, in spite of Elicia's continued game of playing woman and bumping into me in the darkness, giving me the full benefit of her womanly fullness, we made good progress.

It was nearly midnight when Antonio stopped
ahead of us on the trail and held up a hand for
quiet. We hunched in the jungle, unable to see
much more than our hands before our faces. I was
about to ask Antonio why we were stopping when
all hell seemed to break loose on the trail.

First came a high, discordant warbling, as
though a thousand maniacs had just had their
cages rattled. Next was a thundering and thrashing
all around us, not unlike a stampede of heavy
animals. Perhaps elephants or rhinoceroses. We
were struggling to get our weapons lined up when
lights appeared from all around us and the swarm
descended.

Elicia let out a piercing scream. Antonio
bellowed. I was opening my mouth to add to the
general hubbub when strong hands grabbed my
arms and pinned them behind me. I got out one
yell before a rough cloth sack was yanked down
over my head. I felt the cord being tied, a little too
tight for comfort, around my neck. Other hands
were on my legs and feet and torso. One probing
hand even found the bandage over my wound and
sent rivers of pain through my nervous system.

And then, as though a switch had been thrown,
the jungle was silent. We were carried along the
dark trail for the better part of an hour, circling
around to cause us to lose our sense of direction,
then dumped onto hard ground. When the sack
was taken from my head, I found myself tied to
Elicia and Antonio, side by side, in a thatched hut
much like the one Pico had put me in. The ceiling,
however, was considerably higher, and a bunch of
half-naked Indians were standing around us in a
circle. Flame torches were attached to hangers on

the walls, well out from the flammable thatching.

From the circle of Indians stepped an enormous-ly fat man with all sorts of flowered and feathered regalia adorning his body in strategic places. Most of him was exposed and he looked as though he had been wrapped in a macadam parking lot. I had never seen such expanses of human skin on one skeleton.

"I am Botussin," he said in a deep, rich voice with only a touch of growl in it. "I am chief of the Ninca." He motioned toward a tall, lithe brown man who was incredibly handsome, who wore a single eagle feather in his long hair and whose privates were covered by a soft lambskin pouch. "This is my son, Purano, heir to my throne. Now, you will provide us with your names and the rea-sons why you have invaded the Ninca lands, then you will be handed over to our spearchuckers, for execution. You talk now."

He pointed a fat finger at me. Frankly, I was getting a whole lot tired of being tied up and asked to spill my guts about who I was and what I was doing. I could feel Elicia's trembling body against me. Her fear helped me to keep a level head. This fat man meant business and I had damned well bet-ter take that business seriously. He couldn't have cared less about what I was tired of. But I really didn't know where to begin with Botussin, just how much I should tell him. For one thing, I didn't know the sentiments of the Ninca Indians in all that was happening in Nicarxa. Nobody had both-ered to ask them—and that included our in-telligence people whose information had caused me to be sent down here on this wild and woolly caper.

I decided to shorten the distance between what I wanted and what I hoped to get.

"We are here to learn about the cave that Ancio used more than thirty years ago," I said.

I couldn't have gotten more dramatic results if I had plucked a pubic hair out of one of their spearchuckers. That entire circle of half-naked brown men went almost white at the sound of Ancio's name. The chief himself staggered back and looked as though I'd just scored on his huge belly with a sledgehammer. Even the strong, silent son, Purano, appeared stunned, but he held his ground and glowered at me.

"How," the chief began, faltering, stuttering, "how you know of such things? How you know of sacrificial cave, of the devil Ancio?"

There was no reason not to tell him, since the whole country seemed to know of the hermit, Pico, so I told him the whole story, keeping it as short as possible because time was getting more precious by the minute. I down-played the impending war that Don Carlos Italla was plotting from his high place in the clouds and, of course, my role in trying to stop him. I didn't want to complicate the subject for the old chief. As it turned out, he was capable of digesting much more complicated concepts. He was obviously capable of digesting everything.

When I was finished, the circle had quieted down considerably and all the bodies had returned to their original brown hue. The chief motioned to his son and Purano hastily left the hut and came back with a low wooden stool. The chief settled on it and I marveled that he didn't settle all the way to the ground. That stool literally disappeared in the folds of his buttocks. The others, including Purano, stood around with their arms folded, waiting for the chief to continue this absorbing conversation.

"Pico speaks truly," the chief said, "but he knows nothing of that which happened after he left for his hiding place in the mountains. I will tell it all to you, from the beginning."

And he did. Using his soft growl and his still melodious voice to best dramatic effect, he spun a tale of horror that would have done proud any of his ancestors who had stood around campfires in the dead of night frightening the young and the sensitive with horrifying stories of yore.

It seems that Ancio had found an ancient map made up by a long-forgotten ancestor and had used the map to find the entrance of the sacrificial cave. When the tribe had given up human sacrifices more than two hundred years ago, the men had sealed up the cave and had destroyed all visual evidence of its existence, such as maps or descriptions of its locations, even recorded stories of what had taken place there. Even the tribal storytellers were reluctant to mention the cave in the succeeding generations.

But one ancestor had kept a detailed map and this map had been handed down in his own family, kept secret from others in the tribe. More than thirty years ago, an old man on his deathbed summoned Ancio to his side. The old man had no family to give the map to, so he entrusted it to Ancio, forbidding him on pain of death ever to reveal its existence, or to use it to find the cave. According to new tribal gods adopted two hundred years ago, any Ninca who entered the cave, or approached its forbidden entrance—even accidentally—would be burned to a cinder. That was the curse the new gods put on the cave.

The old man died and Ancio went secretly to the cave. He had already begun to think of himself as a god, so he figured he was immune to the spell. Sure enough, he found the cave, went inside and came out again. Not a hair had been scorched, which proved only that the spell of the devil was so strong in him that the new gods couldn't touch him.

In time, Ancio began to take young children there to make sacrifices to the old gods. Or, as Botussin put it, to the devil. Ancio soon enlisted others in his grisly scheme. Before long, the cave became the scene of sexual depravity as Ancio and his friends took young maidens there, abused them in every conceivable fashion and then burned them.

It was when other members of the tribe began to notice smoke rising from Alto Arete that they tumbled to what was really happening to the children and maidens disappearing with regularity from their lands. They didn't know that Pico had discovered Ancio's secret cave and the scene of his depravity. They thought at first that Pico was a victim, having stumbled across his former friend's secret.

But a month after Ancio's disappearance, twenty maidens disappeared from the tribal camp in one night alone. Among them were two of Botussin's daughters, princesses. They were ten and twelve years old. Purano was an infant and was thus spared. One of Botussin's daughters, the twelve-year-old, had the presence of mind to tear small bits of fabric from her garment and drop them on the trail. Botussin and his spearchuckers followed the colorful fragments and found Ancio's encampment on a slope of Mount Toro, where they had apparently stopped to enjoy the maidens prior to going on to the cursed cave.

In the ensuing battle, many of Ancio's friends were killed. He, however, got away with a few of his followers, leaving the map behind. Since the maidens were rescued safe and sound, Botussin did not follow. Ancio never returned, nor did any of his friends.

"If they should ever return," the old chief said in his soft growl, "the spearchuckers will have them. The tribal council has banished them all and has sentenced them to death if they are found."

"Has Pico also been banished and sentenced to death?" I asked. After all, Pico had been Ancio's friend and the tribe never knew why Pico had disappeared.

"No," Botussin said. "Although we knew nothing of what you have told us about Pico, we suspected that he had known of Ancio's activities. After all, his own daughter had disappeared and we all knew that she must have become one of Ancio's victims. Pico has suffered greatly. Although he is not Ninca, he is welcome in Ninca lands if he wishes to return. His enemies are our enemies, his friends our friends. You are obviously his friend or you wouldn't be alive to tell me what you have told me of Pico."

I wanted to clear up that point about Pico eating people who came into his territory, but there was something else of far more importance.

"The map," I said, wondering just how I should phrase the question. "Was it destroyed?"

The old chief took a long time answering that. He looked at the faces around the circle, but there was nothing I could read on those dark, stony faces. His gaze finally fell on his son's face. Slowly, Purano nodded. The chief looked back at me.

"My father was the chief when Ancio was banished from the tribe. It was his decision to keep the map. He entrusted it to me and I shall entrust it to Purano when I go away from life."

"May we see the map?" I asked. I could feel Elicia and Antonio suck in breath at my bold request. Given the knowledge of the Indian's superstitions, or religious beliefs, about that cave, I was a bit surprised myself at my boldness. But a great deal was at stake here.

Once again, the old chief studied his lieutenants' faces and once more it was Purano who gave the nod of assent. The old man responded with a signal and Purano left the hut. The chief nodded toward two guards near the door.

"Remove their bonds," he commanded. "They are friends."

Elicia, whose body had been tense with fear, sagged against me. I glanced at her and her eyes were full of love. I was really turning the girl on and all I was doing was trying to save our lives the best way I knew how. Soon, I would have to do something to kill that love. It couldn't lead anywhere but to a broken heart for her. Or could it? I felt something stir inside me as I gazed into her soft, brown, adoring eyes. It wasn't lust.

While we were still rubbing our wrists and ankles trying to restore circulation, Purano returned with a scroll that looked like the world's oldest high school diploma. It was tied with a length of material that looked like a cow's artery. I learned later that it was.

Botussin dismissed all his lieutenants except Purano and the two of them gently spread the scroll out on the floor of the hut. Antonio, Elicia and I bent over it.

We couldn't make head nor tails of the thing. It

was done in hieroglyphics. Nobody through the
years had thought to transcribe it into more
modern symbols. And there was a fragment of it
missing, in the upper right hand corner. Much of
what was left was so badly stained or faded that it
might as well have been blank.

"None of us can read the map," Botussin explained. "The elder who died without heirs and entrusted the map to Ancio explained its hidden
meanings to him. When he fled, he took the secret
with him."

The map was obviously useless, but there was
still a chance if the old chief were willing to help us.
I put the issue to him.

"I'm afraid the map isn't of much use to us,
Chief Botussin," I said, "and even though Pico has
been to the cave his memories of that night have
been virtually erased. We need your help, though.
Don Carlos plans to touch off a bloody revolution
in just three days. We have no time to search for
the cave. We have to find a way to get up the side
of the mountain. Will you provide warriors to help
us?"

While he was considering the question, Antonio
picked up the map and began to study the weird
symbols and signs.

"You know something of such writings?" the
chief asked.

"In our school, we learned of various Indian
writings and cultures," Antonio said. "These look
familiar to me. May we take the map? I would like
to study it. Perhaps in time. . ."

The old chief sighed.

"You both ask much," he said in a weary voice.
"I cannot help you with warriors in so hopeless a

cause. Already, the most important religious leader of Apalca, a greedy monk named Intenday, has arrived in Nicarxa to meet with Don Carlos. Already, Intenday's caravan moves from the capital to the base of Mount Toro. Guards and soldiers are plentiful. I cannot lend warriors to be killed in attempts to reach the unreachable. You must understand our plight. So many of our maidens were killed by Ancio and his fanatic followers. When Purano was born, we had a large crop of male sons in that year. Today, Purano is past marrying age, yet he has not found a maiden suitable as a bride."

"What about those twenty maidens, including your own daughters, who were saved that night you discovered Ancio's encampment?" I asked.

"They were spoiled before we reached the encampment," Botussin said, matter-of-factly. "They could not become brides, thus could not produce offspring. Certainly none suitable for a prince of Purano's stature."

I thought the old man was being the utter fool, especially since I had noticed Purano giving Elicia a really thorough going-over with his dark, penetrating eyes, but I was in no position to mix in the tribe's cultural affairs. I let that subject drop.

"The map," I said. "May we at least take the map?"

Again Purano nodded and the chief said: "Take the map. Whether it serves your purposes or not, destroy it. I do not wish it to fall into evil hands."

Antonio was almost bowing in thanks to the fat old chief when a sudden thought hit me.

"You say an important religious leader from Apalca is on the way to see Don Carlos."

"Yes, his name is Intenday."

"How do you know such things?"

"We have ways. We keep informed of the activities of Don Carlos Italla. What he does will have devastating effects on the Ninca tribe."

"Will that religious leader be traveling alone, or with a group?"

"He will have his monks with him."

I knew then how to penetrate Don Carlos's tight security. I was ready to leap up and leave the Indian village instantly, but something the chief said held me.

"Why would the activities of Don Carlos have a devastating effect on the Nincas?"

"He hates us," the chief says. "He wants to destroy us. If you can find a way to get to him and not be destroyed in the process, I will supply warriors. Otherwise, we must keep our men here to defend the village when Don Carlos comes to kill us."

I was still puzzled. The old man wasn't making any sense.

"Why would he come to kill you? Why would he single out your tribe?"

"Because he is one of us. Don Carlos is a Ninca."

The puzzlement grew, and it showed clearly on my face. The old chief sighed again, seemed to sink deeper onto the stool and looked to his son for approbation. Purano, the silent, nodded once more.

"Don Carlos Italla," the chief said with a distinct growl, "was once banished and sentenced to death by the Nincas. Don Carlos Italla and the man you know as Ancio are one and the same."

CHAPTER FIVE

I knew I had to go alone. It was not only too dangerous for Elicia and Antonio to go with me, but what I had to do was a one-man job. A job designed for N3, for AXE's top Killmaster.

Meanwhile, we were all nearing exhaustion and I knew that even I would fail without rest.

"What will we do, Senor Carter?" Antonio asked after Botussin and his son had left the hut.

I regarded his handsome, young face in the dim light from the single torch left by the tribal council. He was a courageous young man and I knew that if I told him what was on my mind he'd insist on going along. So would Elicia. She was still sitting close to me, touching me, looking a little disappointed that we weren't still tied together.

"First, we sleep," I said, avoiding Antonio's honest gaze. For some reason, I found it difficult to lie to this young rebel. Just as I found it difficult to be dishonest with Elicia. I could have made love to her on a number of occasions, especially back there in the jungle when she was bathing, and singing to herself, just behind that wall of vines.

"All right," Antonio said, lying back on his pallet and covering himself with the coarse blanket Botussin's servant had brought us. "But we must leave at first light. We must find a way up the mountain and we must do it soon."

"True," I said, lying back also and watching Elicia settle herself on her pallet right beside me. "Too true. But now, we sleep."

Antonio insisted that the torch be left on for a time so he could study that infernal map. Elicia clearly showed her disappointment. I knew she was waiting for darkness to slip under my blanket. Where would all my honesty with her be then? Would I refuse her again? I didn't know. Frankly, there was a lot of disappointment of my own when Antonio asked that the torch remain lighted.

The girl was getting to me. That song in the jungle kept running through my mind: "When my love is near me, I am like the rose; Budding, blossoming, flowering, More than my love knows." I could hear her sweet, bell-clear voice singing it. I could even feel her soft body touching me, rubbing against me.

And it was more than the song and the voice and the physical touching. The girl was touching me in other places, deep in my soul. Of all the women I had known in my uncountable escapades as N3, few had strummed those deep chords. There had been some I had loved, some I had merely dallied with—even been dishonest with. They were all different. Or, to put it another way, Elicia was different.

The open honesty that I could see readily in An-

tonio was there in spades in Elicia. In spite of all
that happened to her, she was truly the innocent,
the unsullied, the pure. That was because everything that had happened to her had happened only
to her flesh. Nothing had harmed her soul, her
goodness. And what she wanted from me was not
a mere meeting of the flesh. My flesh was ready,
God knew; it had been ready since that first night
on the trail when she had overcome her aversion to
the rapings and had begun to touch me, subtly, in
the dark. But as yet my soul wasn't ready for that
honest and pure meeting with this precious girl.

It was getting there, though.

With such thoughts in my mind, and with the
torch still fizzing brightly on the wall of the
thatched hut, I fell into a deep sleep. I remember
glancing over at Elicia just before falling asleep.
She was gazing at me, her eyes bright and clear, her
lips slightly parted, her bosom heaving with passion. Whether she knew it or not, we were making
passionate love in that moment. It was a good
thought to sleep on.

Three hours later, to the minute, I snapped
awake. I had programmed my mind to come alert
in three hours. Sometimes, it works, sometimes it
doesn't. This night, it worked.

The torch was out and Antonio was snoring
lightly, but Elicia was as silent as stone. Was she
faking sleep? Would she follow me from the hut? I
waited, then heard her deep, heavy breathing. She
was sound asleep.

I made my way to Purano's hut, having been
told that the son slept to his father's right hand.
The chief's hut was unmistakable, clearly the larg-
est and most elaborate in the tribe. I crept in and

gently shook Purano's shoulder.

"It's me, Nick Carter," I said. "I have dangerous business in the valley and I don't want to disturb your father. But I want a promise from him—from both of you."

I'm certain he nodded there in the blackness, unwilling to speak. Finally, he muttered an almost inaudible, "what is the promise?"

"Keep the young people here," I said. "What I must do, I must do alone. If they follow me, they'll only endanger themselves and perhaps the whole plan. Will you keep them here, keep them safe until it's all over?"

After a long silence, he asked: "What will you do?"

"I'm going to join Intenday, the Apalcan religious leader, on his way to meet with Don Carlos. I don't know just how, but I've got to try. We don't have time to search for that ancient sacrificial cave. I may not even have enough time to do what I'm planning."

"You go to Alto Arete?"

"If I can."

"And then?"

Truth to tell, I hadn't really given that part a lot of thought. I had begun to plan ways to infiltrate the contingent of the religious leader from Apalca the minute I had heard of him going there. Somehow, some way, I would kill Don Carlos Italla once I got to Alto Arete. Just how, I didn't know right then.

"It's a military secret," I said, grinning at myself in the dark hut. "Will you keep Antonio and Elicia here?"

"If I succeed," I said, "I'll come back for them. If I don't succeed, I think you and everyone else on the island will know about it. Thank you—and thank your father—for all your help."

I could tell he was nodding from the sound of his head on his rough pillow. I got up and left the hut, wondering why in thunder I was doing such a foolish and dangerous thing for these foreigners in this foreign land. If I merely walked to the ocean and stole a boat and sailed it to Florida, who could blame me? Certainly not David Hawk, who would understand that the odds were clearly against me. Not the President, who would also know that my mission had become suicidal. Not Elicia and Antonio, who would marvel at my foolish courage when they awoke and learned from Purano where I was going. Then who would blame me? Nick Carter would blame me. He always had and he always would. I would blame, myself, and that is blame that I've never learned to live with.

Even so, I was a lonely and slightly terrified man as I made my way down the jungle trail from the Ninca lands. Some of my thoughts remained behind with Elicia, wondering if she had awakened and found me gone. Wondering also what it might have been like if Antonio hadn't been studying that cryptic map and had put out the torch before I fell asleep.

I knew what it would have been like. Elicia would have crept beneath my blanket. Her soft, shapely body would have molded to mine under that blanket. Flesh would have responded to flesh. Soul would have responded to soul. And then. . .

I started to run on the trail, knowing that it is impossible to run away from love.

From the lookout point, I could see as much as I needed to see in the Reina Valley. The campfires

of the Cuban Marines had burned low, glowing
like red eyes in the blanket of darkness below. But
farther down the valley, perhaps four miles from
the Marine encampment, was something new.

Campfires blazed there as the night grew colder.
Through my binoculars, I could see the shadows of
hooded monks moving about the new camp, tending the fires. In the center of the new camp, fire-
light dancing on its ornate walls, was the tent of
Intenday, the religious leader from Apalca. There
were no sentries that I could see, but they could
have been hidden in the jungle around the encampment. In a ring around the encampment, almost
beyond the glow of the fires, were carts and oxen.
The beasts were presumably asleep, standing with
heads low to the ground, but not grazing. Lucky
for me the travelers were using oxen and not jeeps;
otherwise, they'd already have reached the base
camp of the Cuban Marines.

The timing on this was perfect so far. I had
caught up with Intenday and his contingent of
monks just hours before they would break camp
and make the final jaunt to the base of Mount
Toro. If I had succumbed to Elicia's charms, or if
my automatic mental alarm hadn't awakened me, I
would have missed them altogether. Even as it was,
there was no guarantee that my plan would work—
and I still had no plan as to what I would do once
I was on top of the huge mountain.

I had virtually forgotten my wound on the long
trek down from Ninca lands. Old Pico's poultice of
mosses and herbs had done a miraculous job and I
toyed with the idea of taking his secret back to the
States with me, if I ever got there. I discarded the
idea, knowing the reception it would receive from
the AMA. After thirty or forty years of testing, it

would be discarded or shunted to the medical attic where it would never heal a single wound. Oh well.

Before leaving the lookout, I checked my personal arsenal. I had strapped four gas bombs to the insides of my thighs, to go along with the one in the lamb's wool pouch behind my testicles. Hugo, my faithful and reliable stiletto, was in his leather sheath along my left forearm. Wilhelmina, the luger, was taped to my back and I had six extra clips taped around the bandage on my side wound.

I was as ready as I ever would be. I crushed out my cigarette and buried the butt deep, just in case someone came along and saw the NC in gold.

The binoculars hadn't lied about the sentries. There were none. I slipped through the final section of jungle and peered at the firewatchers who were still piling on wood. Dawn was threatening to break over the top of the mountain dead ahead of us. I had to hurry.

From my cover at the edge of the clearing, I singled out a monk who looked about my height. I watched him closely, studying his movements. It was impossible to see his face because of the dim light and the elaborate hood that projected out beyond his head. That wasn't a concern. Once inside his hood and robe, my face would be equally difficult to see. To make certain, I dug my hands in the soft, black dirt of the jungle floor and smeared my face with it.

And then I moved forward just as the monk who was my height moved away from the ring of campfires to search for new firewood.

Patience is very much a part of my work, but I found that I had little of it as the monk kept stopping to peer at the ground and then in my direction. Could he see me hiding there at the edge of the clearing? No, impossible. I was behind a thick bush, watching him from the bottom edge. And the dawn light was still so dim that he couldn't have seen me from twenty paces away if I had been standing in the open.

Slowly, the monk made his way in my direction. When he came within those twenty paces, I was ready to make my move. I slid Hugo into my hand, knowing that the monk's death had to come quietly. He advanced within ten paces, still not enough, and I felt my muscles go taut, waiting, waiting.

The monk stopped, leaned over and plucked a piece of firewood from the dark ground. He had only four or five slender pieces in his arms, but I was afraid he'd go back with them and then find a new area to search. Before long, it would be too light for me to shift my position to intercept his line of search.

He was a slow one, that monk. He stood there examining that piece of firewood the way he might have gazed at a piece of the true cross. I was about ready to start cursing him under my breath, then I held back the curse. I was about to kill this man, this total stranger to me. The least I could do was hold back the curses, even if my heart wasn't bubbling over with compassion. And yet, compassion was there. This man was guilty of nothing. He was a simple (and perhaps simple-minded) follower who happened to be in the wrong place at the wrong time. For him, that is. For me, and for the honest people of Nicarxa, this man doing everything right. Slowly, but right.

He came within five paces, still too far away, searched the dark ground, glanced back at the fires and his roaming comrades, then stopped cold. I was sweating with tension and my muscles were beginning to knot from being held taut so long. I took a deep breath, relaxed all my muscles, felt relief ripple through my body, then poised again to leap on the unsuspecting monk.

He looked in my direction, then scanned the dark ground near the jungle wall. He took another step, and another.

I leaped out so quickly that even I was surprised. I hit him with my body and he went down like a structure of straw. Even as my left hand was searching for his mouth to keep him from crying out, my right hand was bringing Hugo around in a wide arc. Both hands did their work simultaneously.

There was no cry. Only a soft grunt signalled the death of the monk. The stiletto made a wide, gaping gash of his throat, and warm blood spilled over my own chest. I lay on the ground on top of the monk, my left hand still on his mouth to make certain no final death cry would escape. He was soft as wet clay, and I knew he was dead. It was then that the compassion bubbled over and I wished him back to life.

It took only a few minutes to drag the monk into the jungle and strip him of his robe and hood. I barely noticed his shaved head, but was struck by the rough, unbleached shorts he wore under his religious attire. Those must smart on hot days, I thought. He also wore crude leather sandals and had a crude wooden cross on a cheap chain around his neck. I left the shorts and the cross on his body, and slipped into his robe and sandals. I raised the cowl until it virtually obstructed my vison, but hid my face.

I gathered up the fallen sticks of firewood and began looking for more, taking my sweet old time about it. Fortunately, I had watched the monk long enough to know that he had a specific fire to tend. I looked over, saw that the fire was burning low, and started off to put the firewood on it. Just beyond the campfire was Intenday's huge tent. I gave it a covert inspection as I stepped up and carefully put the firewood on the fire. There was a soft light in there, as though the holy man were awakening to start the day's journey.

"More quickly, Nuyan," a voice from my left called out softly. "We must build the fires for the breakfast. Move more quickly, if that is possible, you slow mule, you."

I turned slowly, but not all the way, to see who was speaking. Another monk, short and squat, was piling a huge load of wood on the next fire. I could see part of his chubby face and he was smiling.

"That's right, Nuyan," the monk said, laughter in his voice, "keep going at your own pace and the Iman will have a cold breakfast. And you, my slow-paced friend, will find yourself scrubbing the kitchens at home for a month. Try to make haste, won't you?"

I said nothing. Supposing the monk Nuyan was a mute? Supposing he had a lisp or a nasal twang or a different Spanish accent. Silence and slowness were my best friends now. I moved away from the fire and went seriously about the business of gathering firewood. It wouldn't do me any good to draw attention to Nuyan by having the Iman eat a cold breakfast.

Things went well after that. I got the fire going furiously, though I was worried about that breakfast bit. Did Nuyan have to fix the religious leader's breakfast? If so, I would have to get too close to the man and he'd certainly notice that I wasn't the real Nuyan.

However, by the time I'd brought back my third load of firewood, the servants were already out preparing breakfast in great black pots. Along the road, other monks were readying the carts and oxen, getting them hitched for the short run to the base camp. Tents around the Iman's big tent were being struck and folded.

"Come, Nuyan," the chubby monk said from behind me. "We get to sleep while the Iman eats. Come, you slowpoke."

I turned, slowly of course, and saw the chubby monk joining the other fire tending monks near the base of a huge palm tree. The monks were stretching out on the ground and curling up inside their robes. I circled around to avoid the chubby man who was so talkative to Nuyan, picked out a spot and pretended to sleep.

But sleep wasn't a part of my program just then. I'd had precious little of it and wanted to drop off into dreamland, but I kept my eyes on the monks to see if I could spot weapons among them. I didn't. I did see Intenday, though, when he came out to warm his hands before the fire.

He was a small, wiry, insignificant-looking man in a bright red robe and hood to match. He pushed back the hood and I saw a brown bald head and an enormous nose. But his eyes were so large and glistening that the corpse-like ugliness of the man was soon forgotten. There was no benevolence in that man and I wondered about the people of Apalca and why they would choose a holy man who obviously was so full of greed and evil; and completely devoid of compassion. At least in those great, penetrating, conniving eyes.

A half hour later, the camp was struck, the Iman had his breakfast tucked away in his stomach and the call went out to the oxen. The carts began to roll.

"Come on, slugabed Nuyan," the chubby monk called across to me. "Rustle your bones. Time to go."

I got up and followed the others. Leading the caravan were the oxcarts. Following them was the ornate wagon carrying Intenday and his lieutenants. Other monks strung out in a double line on the narrow road. The firewatching monks were last, straggling along single file. That was fine with me. I held back, waiting for the fat monk to fall in line, then brought up the rear.

It was, I learned, the customary position for Nuyan. He always brought up the rear. The monk directly in front of me turned occasionally to smile, as though he were giving encouragement to a dim-witted child. I bent my head and tried to pull it deeper into the hood.

The sun was up full when we reached the base camp. Ahead, I could see a group of Marine guards letting the oxcarts go past. Then, a group of officers came out of the main building to greet Intenday's carriage.

Leading the officers was my old nemesis: Col. Ramon Vasco. I checked my weapons under the robe. In spite of my heavy sweating, everything was in place. But I still felt a tremor of fear and excitement through my body. What if the man recognized me? No, he was paying no attention to the humble monks. All his attentions were centered on the holy man in the carriage.

As I waited at the end of the line for the officers

and the religious leaders to observe the customary amenities, the chubby monk came back to stand alongside me. I sucked in my breath, and my head, and pretended to be watching something back down the road.

"You're quieter than usual, Nuyan," the gabby one said. "Did you lose your tongue during the long night tending the fires?"

I shook my head no, hoping that was another of Nuyan's habits. It apparently was. The fat monk went on jabbering about how sleepy he was, how slow I was, how hot the sun was, how high the mountain was, how glad he'd be when we reached the top and had decent food. He talked enough for eight monks and I was happy to let him ramble. Suddenly, I could feel him staring at me.

"Something is wrong, Nuyan," he said, stepping closer. "Come, turn and look at me. Tell me what's wrong."

Away from him, I twitched the muscles of my left forearm and popped Hugo into my hand. If this man discovered I wasn't Nuyan, I would have to kill him before he set up the alarm. With luck, I could be a hundred yards into the jungle before the others figured out what the hell had happened.

In that moment, as I felt the monk tugging at the sleeve of the robe and my hand was tightening on the stiletto's helt, the Iman's wagon began to roll forward and the oxtenders let out a loud "Yo-ho, yo-ho."

"Come on, slowpoke," the fat monk said, tugging harder. "Try to keep up. The trail gets rough now."

Old chubby took his usual place near the head of the line of firetenders. I realized then that even these lowly monks had a pecking order and a kind of protocol of position. My position was last in line. Somehow, I wasn't offended or humbled by that.

After an hour, the oxcarts and the leader's carriage had to be left behind. Monks carried the Iman on a chair attached to long poles until the trail got so steep that the wiry man had to actually walk. Even so, two of his lieutenants were right beside him, gripping his skinny arms and helping him up the narrow trail.

We reached the first gap in the trail about ten o'clock. The sun was hot above us and not even the stiff breeze from the ocean helped to dissipate the heat. Sweat was showing through the robes of the monks ahead of me, and through the uniforms of the Cuban Marine guards who manned the station ahead.

I spotted movement high above and saw that a basket on a rope was being lowered by monks in red robes and green hoods. These were the special monks, from the private order of Don Carlos Italla. There were four of them working a winch at a tiny building on a ledge a hundred feet above where the mountain trail ended. I held back, observing what was happening, watching the Cuban guards to see if they were searching anyone. There were no searches.

The Iman was taken up first, then his lieutenants. The Cuban guards observed the operations closely, looking into the face of each monk as he was taken aboard the basket and hoisted up by the rope and winch to the next level. I looked up again and saw that the Iman and the monks who had already been raised were already moving along a trail up there. This was only the first of several points where the trail had been blasted away and where we would be hoisted to a new level. It was also the first of several points where Cuban guards would get a good look at my face.

Well, it was nothing to worry about. They couldn't know me, couldn't know that I was not really Nuyan, the slowpoke, the slow-witted. If they wondered about the dirt on my face, they'd just have to accept the fact that Nuyan was also untidy.

When the others had been hoisted and the basket was being lowered for me—for the last monk in the procession—I held my breath and waited. There were six guards at this point in the trail. Two of them had already gotten a good look at my face and hadn't shown any suspicion. I had given them a beatific smile, befitting a humble monk. I waited, mentally checking the whereabouts of my luger, my gas bombs and, of course, Hugo. I had calmed all earlier tensions and felt quite at ease as the basket nudged the ground and a Cuban Marine signalled for me to sit in it.

The basket was actually part of an old wicker chair that had had the legs sawn off. An extra piece of wicker was hinged to fit across the front, to keep the occupant from tumbling out. The Marine guard latched the piece in place and signalled to the monks above. They began turning the crank on the winch and I felt myself being raised into space.

The view was incredible from this level. I could see the capital several miles to the south. I could see the ocean on either side of the island, east and west. When I had been raised fifty feet, I could also see the base camp of the Marine detachment at the foot of the mountain. The wind was higher now and it was flipping the robe and hood around with cracking sounds.

The winch worked with unsettling creaking sounds above me. I looked up through the web of ropes holding the chair and saw the green-hooded monks at the little station house on the upper trail. They were smiling down at me, knowing I was the last of this particular party, knowing that they could rest now, perhaps have a little wine and swap monk stories at their tiny station. I was only ten feet from the top.

At that moment, the wind caught my hood and whipped it back over my shoulders before I could catch it.

The winch stopped.

I snatched my hood back in place and looked up, wondering why the winch had stopped. The four monks were chattering agitatedly above me, pointing to my head, reaching under their own hoods. The wind was whipping me and the chair about. I was hanging suspended in mid-air, ninety feet from the watching Marines below, only ten feet from the winching station and safety.

Why had they stopped?

And then it hit me. They had seen my head and I had a full head of dark brown hair.

Only then did the significance of Nuyan's shaved head come to me. Only then did I recall more sharply the brown bald head of Intenday.

Monks in this part of the world, I knew then, had no hair. It had all been shaved off. I was obviously an imposter.

The monks above me were still chattering among themselves, trying to decide what to do next. They obviously weren't empowered to make many decisions on their own. I could hear them calling for the monks of Intenday's party, to come and identify me. With my luck, the fat monk would be the first one to show up, confirm that I was not Nuyan, and order the green-hooded monks to drop me like a hot potato.

I looked around wildly, inspecting the wall of the mountain not more than a few feet away. There were narrow ledges against the facing of the rock mountain. There were also shiny bits of metal and I remembered being told that those bits of metal were all over the mountainside, off the trails, and that they were coated with poison.

While the shouting continued above me, and the Cuban Marine guards below me were alerted that something was amiss, I began to arch my body back and forth, like a child in a harmless playground swing. If the winch gave way from the extra pressure, or if the green-hooded monks suddenly released the lock on the winch, it was all over for me. I kept arching my back, swinging in closer to the mountain.

On the fifth swing, I was nearing a ledge that was perhaps ten feet wide and about ten inches deep. Below that were other ledges at about ten and twenty-foot intervals.

On the sixth swing, my feet touched the ledge. On the seventh, I was able to make a slight purchase with my toes. To give myself a better chance, I kicked off Nuyan's sandals and heard them clatter down the rocky mountain, knocking loose pebbles down on the Marine guards.

"Bring him up," I heard the fat monk scream from above.

"Drop him down, drop him down," another monk yelled.

I had just pushed away from the mountain and was at the apex of another swing out into space when I looked down and saw the Cuban Marines

aiming their rifles up at me. I had to make the ledge
on this try or I wouldn't have another chance. Even
so, where would I go from there? I tried not to
think of that. I put everything I had into that
swing, bearing down so hard on the wicker chair
and tugging so hard on the ropes as I arched my
body that I was certain something had to snap—
the ropes, the lock on the winch, the winch itself.

Bullets were now plunking into the rocks. My
feet landed on the ledge and I dug in my toes for
maximum purchase. I felt the chair drop away behind me and knew that it was all between me, the
ledge and gravity. And, of course, the poison-
coated steel scraps on the ledge.

The wall above the ledge bulged out from the
mountain, giving me little room. My feet had adequate purchase on the ledge, but I had to double
over fast to keep from slamming my shoulders in
the bulge of rock and being knocked back into
space. In one swift, writhing movement, I curled
my body and landed on the ledge on my right side.
My hands and feet grasped for holds and, as the
wind still ripped at my robe and hood, I felt myself
settle onto the solid surface.

I had made it, just barely, but there were other
problems. Bullets were smacking into the outcropping of rock above me, sending splinters of rock in
a shower all over me. A ricochet could easily do me
in. And I could feel the sharp pricks of the metal
shreds beneath my body as I clung to the ledge.
Fortunately, the two thicknesses of cloth—the robe
and my own clothes—had so far kept the metal
from puncturing my skin. So far.

The bulge of rock above me proved to be a salva-
tion for now. The clustered monks above couldn't
see me. Even if they had guns and would let down

their religious tenets long enough to fire them, they had no clear line of vision. For the moment, if a ricochet didn't get me, I was safe.

Slowly, carefully, I moved about on the narrow ledge and plucked up the bits of sharp metal. I flung them over the side, hoping the wind would catch them and drive them into the Marines still firing from below. The Marines also had no clear line of vision, but their bullets were just as dangerous as if they had me as an easy target.

The firing ceased just about the time I had located and discarded the last chunk of poisoned metal. I stretched out on my stomach and gazed over the ledge. I could see the roof of the small station below, but couldn't see the Marines. I knew, though, that the guards had already sent word down the mountain via walkie-talkie that an imposter had made it this far. Marines would be coming up in force.

I spotted another ledge a dozen feet below me and to the left of the point where the winch stood above me. I worked my way to the extreme end of my ledge, tossing over metal scraps as I went, and prepared to drop down to that next ledge. The sunlight caught hunks of sharp metal down there and gave me fair warning. I had no sandals now; dropping down there barefoot would be certain suicide.

An idea came. I took off Nuyan's robe and hood, and began to tear them into strips. Working slowly and purposefully, wondering what the guards below and the monks above were plotting, I wrapped my feet, hands, buttocks, thighs and hands with the heavy garb of the monk. If I had had more material, I would have wrapped myself up like a mummy, but I didn't so I would have to take more risks with the sharp metal and the poison than I wanted to take, but there was no other way.

Sure enough, when I dropped to the next ledge, my left foot landed on a huge chunk of metal. I eased up quickly and the metal didn't make it through to skin. And I had made it to the ledge without being observed from above or below. I knew this because the guards were still firing sporadically, and their bullets were going to that outcropping of rock that had been above me on the first ledge.

This second, lower ledge was about thirty feet wide and a foot deep. I cleared it of metal and worked my way to the westernmost end where I dropped to a third ledge only six feet down. I was still more than seventy feet above the trail and was running out of ledges that would keep my momentum to the west, away from the guard station.

I found a small cave on the third ledge, but it would do no good to hide out in there. Even if they didn't find me, I would soon starve. I had already decided that I couldn't wait for darkness to cover my escape from this rock wall of a mountain. Darkness would not be my friend and ally up here. If I didn't miss my footing in the dark, I would certainly fall prey to the ubiquitous metal shards if I couldn't spot them ahead of time.

In fifteen minutes, though, I had worked my way down four more ledges, to a point about thirty feet above the trail and a hundred yards to the west of the Marine station. The Marines were still taking potshots at the first ledge and, above, the four green-hooded monks manning the winch had filled the wicker chair with an enormous rock and had lowered it ten feet. They were swinging it back and forth, trying to hit whoever might be hiding there.

Of course, no one was.

Intenday and his group had apparently gone on up the trail, working their way to the top where plans of war would be discussed with Don Carlos Italla. Following this incident of the imposter and the killing of the real Nuyan, I had no doubts as to the outcome of that discussion. Don Carlos would get his support and he would signal from his cloud-ringed mountaintop in two days for the bloody sport to begin.

Once again, my efforts to head off trouble had only fueled the fires of war and made my own task more difficult. Perhaps I'm a firetender by nature.

While I was resting at my last point, thirty feet above the trail, I heard a terrible hubub below and looked down to see Colonel Vasco and a whole company of Marines scrambling up the trail. The final passage to the trail was a gradual slope. I wouldn't have to jump it. If it weren't for the metal slivers and the Marines coming up the trail, I could slide down it and run like hell for a time. Eventually, though, I knew I would have to come face to face with the Marines. Unless I wanted to take an even bigger chance with the metal scraps and hot-foot it down the mountain slope to the west.

I crammed myself back against the wall at the back of my last ledge and let the Marines go streaming past below. Soon, I knew, they would have the monks lower the basket, put an armed Marine in it and winch him up to the ledge where I'd gotten off. At that time, the search would fan out and they'd find me. There were more than a hundred of them up on the trail now, and I couldn't be more than two hundred yards from the station at the gap in the trail.

I remained hidden, not even watching the

Marines at their latest activity. After ten minutes, I heard one of them trudging back down the trail, apparently going after climbing equipment to supplement the winch. I waited another five minutes, surveyed the slope beneath me for metal scraps and then went over.

Five metal scraps caught in the wrappings, but I plucked them out and sent them flying over the trail. I reached the trail, undetected I was sure, and began running down toward the base camp. It had taken us two hours of climbing to reach this point; I figured I could run back down it in about fifteen minutes. I figured wrong.

As I made a turn around the side of the mountain, I came face to face with Col. Ramon Vasco. He was leaning against the mountain, smoking a cigarette. The cigarette dangled untended between his heavy lips. Across his middle, pointing directly at me, was a loaded Volska automatic rifle.

"We meet again, Senor Carter," he said, spitting out the words and smiling with a ruthlessness that made my bowels churn. "This time, I know who you are. You can't fool me with stories about being on special assignment for Captain Rodrigues. And this time, you will not squirrel away into thin air."

"It would seem that way," I said, retaining my outward glibness. Inside, I was in riot, trying to decide which of my weapons to go for first. It had to be Wilhemina, the luger. I was too far away to be effective with Hugo, and poor old Pierre would be too slow for his quick trigger-finger. "What's keeping you? Why don't you shoot?"

His smile broadened and became even more ruthless looking, if possible.

"Patience, Mr. Carter," he said. "You've exhibited a great deal of it in infiltrating my ranks and then concealing yourself among these humble men of God. I will be the one to kill you, make no mistake about that. First, I wish to ask you a few questions."

"Go ahead." I was inching forward, hoping he wouldn't notice but knowing he would. He did.

"Don't move any farther," he snapped, "or we forget the questions and toss your body over the side of the mountain. When you are questioned, it will be by experts. Take my word for it, Mr. Carter. When they are finished with you, we will know everything you know, and more. You will talk as you have never talked before."

"You have ways," I said, using the old cliche in a mocking manner.

"Many, many ways. Now, move to the outer edge of the trail and pass by me. We will go down to the base camp now."

"How did you know I wasn't still up on that ledge?" I asked as we trudged along single file down the trail.

"I didn't. But I have witnessed your miracles before, Senor Carter. This time, I decided to detach myself from the scene and hope that the thin air you disappeared into would be occupied by me. And it was, much to your misfortune."

At a turn in the trail, I saw a squad of Marines far ahead. We would catch up to them in a matter of seconds. Thirty or forty at the most. It would surely be all over for me then. I might have a chance against one armed man, but not a squad of them. I stumbled and stopped. Colonel Vasco stopped behind me.

"What is it? Why do you stop?"

I turned and showed him the blood on my chest. It was Nuyan's blood, but the colonel didn't know it. I leaned against the side of the mountain and let my body sag as though weak. I put my hand to my face and bent over.

"A piece of metal," I said, gasping out the words for effect. "When I dropped down on a ledge up there, a piece of metal cut through my clothes. I feel sick. Weak."

The last words had come slowly, far apart, in a slurred voice. I heard the colonel swear and knew that he was certain the poisoned metal would cheat him out of his brutal interrogation and final disposition of my body. He wanted me for his own, wanted the pleasure of seeing me tortured, the pleasure of pulling the trigger to blast the last remnants of life from my body.

I sagged further and reached out my hand, as though seeking relief from my building agonies.

"Son of a bitch," he grumbled, as he moved forward to take my outstretched hand. "You can't die here. You. . ."

Hugo flashed in the air and caught the colonel in the throat. His automatic rifle plummeted to the ground and he let out a cry that could have been heard all the way to Miami. When I had wrapped my right hand, I had kept the stiletto clutched in my fingers. But my aim hadn't been as accurate as it should. I withdrew the weapon and plunged it in again, this time in his chest, hoping to pierce his heart.

He fell, slowly, just as the squad of Marines down the trail broke into a run. They had seen me attack the colonel. Two of them had veered off to one side and were on their knees, taking aim to kill the colonel's attacker.

I had no choice, I leaped over the side of the trail and slid on my belly down into the jungle thicket, knowing that it was full of poison-coated metal.

CHAPTER SIX

Bullets swept the hillside like a wave of water before a high wind. I leaped to my wrapped feet and made a twisting, turning dash down the mountain. Although I was out of sight from the Marine squad above, their weapons were sweeping the underbrush that was no protection from steel-jacketed bullets.

Small trees, limbs and bushes all around me were cracking and flashing from the rain of bullets. Clusters of leaves literally exploded in my face. I could see the bits of metal that obviously had been dropped on the mountainside by an aircraft, and knew that I was stepping on those bits as I ran helter-skelter down through the thickening jungle. I could only hope that the wrappings would hold out, would absorb the penetrating shards.

Ironically, it was the existence of the poisoned metal bits that enabled me to get away from the squad of Marines on the trail above. They didn't have their lives at stake, weren't as desperate as I was, so they had no intentions of following me into that sea of death and danger. I zig-zagged across the downward slope, found an old Indian trail and made a beeline straight to the valley floor.

When I was out of the area that had been seeded with the poisoned metal, I found a stream and sat down to rest. The wound in my side had come open during the flight and the pain of it was growing unbearable. There was also something in the wrapping on my right foot, a pebble perhaps that was pressing against the sole of my foot.

I washed the jungle dirt from my face and took off the filthy bindings. I checked the bandage over my side wound, found it soaked in blood, but didn't dare remove it. Pico's healing herbs and mosses were still there, doing their magic.

When I had finished washing, I lay on the bank to rest and let my side stop bleeding. I hadn't found a pebble in the wrapping on my right foot, but I soon forgot about that. After resting, I got up and continued on down the Indian path until it faded into jungle. I picked lines of least resistance and, following the sun which I could see at uneven intervals, made my way ever westward toward Ninca lands. With luck, I would be there by dusk. Perhaps now I'd be able to convince Chief Botussin that he'd better lend help with his full complement of warriors. We could at least get to the capital, warn of the coming revolution, and stir up enough action among rebels and government forces there to put a crimp in Don Carlos Italla's plans. If we did our work well, his signal from the cloud-wreathed summit of Alto Arete might not have its full sting; the revolution might fail.

It was a slim hope, but my only one right then. I had thought of going back up to where I had stashed my radio and remaining supplies, where I could hopefully impress on David Hawk, or others at AXE that, unless they came through with support, two more third world nations would slip out of our grasp to the tune of a great deal of bloodshed. Recalling my last effort, I gave up on the idea. It would take too many precious hours and, I was convinced, would prove fruitless.

I hadn't gone a mile through the jungle, though, when I began to feel a throbbing in my right foot. I ignored it for a time, but stopped when I came to the stream where Elicia had taken her bath and had sung her sweet song. I sat on the bank and twisted my foot around to look at the bottom. It was filthy from black jungle dirt, so I dipped it into the stream to wash it off.

The sting of the water was like a hot poker on my foot. I pulled my foot up again and saw the tiny pinprick in the soft part of my arch. The redness and the swelling told me the worst. There had been no pebble in that wrapping.

There had been a piece of the tainted steel, and it had punctured my skin.

I nearly panicked then, knowing from what I'd been told that I probably had little time to live. First, I would grow woozy and weak, then I would become faint, finally going into delerium, then coma, then death.

With all the strength I had, I pulled the foot to my mouth and began to suck blood from the pinprick wound. Not much came out, but I spat it into the stream. An idea hit and I used Hugo to cut an X-mark through the wound. Blood flowed copiously and I sucked and spat until I began to feel nausea. It wasn't enough. The poison had already started working its way up my leg.

The second idea hit and, even though I didn't hold out much hope for it, it was certainly worth a try. I removed the bandage from my side and scooped out a portion of the now putrid poultice Pico had applied to my bullet wound.

Working patiently and diligently in spite of growing panic, I worked the grisly concoction of moss and herbs deep into the wound on my foot. I wrapped it with my handkerchief, rested for another fifteen minutes, then tested it out. The foot hurt like hell when I stood on it, but I no longer felt wooziness. I knew that, for the poultice to work—if it had any power left—I would have to rest there several hours and let its healing powers seep into my blood along with the poison, but there was no time for that. I had to find Botussin and convince him of the need for hasty action, for a smallscale war, if possible.

The more I walked, the greater the foot hurt. By the time I was within sight of Ninca lands, I was more than exhausted. My side wound was bleeding profusely and the poison had worked its way to my hips. I felt a kind of paralysis setting in there. But I plugged along, stumbling, falling; passing out for short stretches. At times, my mind drifted and I could see myself plunging headlong down another ravine. This time, I knew, Pico wouldn't be there to rescue me. I was miles from his hermitage up on the side of the mountain.

It was late afternoon when I found the final trail leading to Botussin's camp. In just over twenty four hours, at dusk tomorrow, Don Carlos Italla would walk to the edge of his lair in the clouds and send the signal to start the revolution. There was no doubt in my mind that he'd gain the full support of Intenday and his followers from Apalca.

I literally crawled into the Ninca encampment and, just before passing out, saw Purano and two of his warriors coming toward me. The two warriors had spears in their hands and I thought then that something had gone wrong and they were now ready to turn me over to the spear chuckers.

At that point, I really didn't give a damn. In fact, I would welcome the sweet rest that would come from death by any means.

It was dark when I awoke in the now familiar hut. I opened my eyes and saw one lighted torch on the opposite wall. I swiveled my eyes to my right and there was Elicia, sitting cross-legged beside me, a damp cloth in her hands. She had been applying the cloth to my fevered brow. Near her stood Antonio and Purano, watching anxiously to see if I would speak or merely give out a death rattle.

But Pico's poultice had done its job, in spite of my failure to cooperate with its healing powers. I felt a bit stronger, but still was unable to rise on my own. Antonio and Purano, against Elicia's wishes, helped me to a sitting position. Botussin entered then and sat on his familiar stool.

With great effort, I told of what had happened to me since leaving the Ninca lands in the middle of last night. When I was finished, they were all convinced that we had lost. There was no way to penetrate Don Carlos Italla's fortress, no way to halt the revolution that would come at dusk tomorrow, about twenty hours away. Antonio had news that had excited them all during the day, but now he wasn't certain.

"I understand some of the symbols on the map," he said, "but most are so faint that none of us could read them. With Purano's help, and a few of his warriors, we made it to the general vicinity of the cave's entrance, but it could be in one of several hollows on the side of the mountain. And there are guerillas and Cuban Marines scouting that area. We were nearly discovered a half-dozen times, and escaped just in time. I'm afraid. . ."

He sounded so defeated, so desolate. I had no ideas to cheer him, so I said nothing, unwilling to let them hear the note of defeatism in my own voice. I lay back down, wanting sleep and rest, but afraid to waste anymore time.

"We have to try again," I said. "With what you've made out on the map, we at least know the general location of the cave. We can search all night, avoid the patrols of the guerillas and the Marines, and maybe get lucky."

"Lucky the way we've been all along?" Antonio asked with a trace of bitteriness in his voice.

"Luck has a way of changing," I said wearily, unable to feel the optimism that my tone implied. "It's time it swung around in our direction."

"We will help with warriors for such a venture," Botussin said. He had listened to our repartee and had decided that I was right. It was worth another try. "Purano will lead our warriors. They will be at your disposal, Senor Carter."

For the first time since my return, I noticed that Elicia, though attentive to my needs, hadn't been regarding me with such open adoration. She didn't seem to need to be near me, to touch me often. I

soon discovered why. She was sitting quite close to
Purano and he was regarding her with a tenderness
that I quickly recognized as budding romance. I
remembered then what Botussin had told me during our initial discussion, when we had all been tied
together in his council hut the first night we came
here. "So many of our maidens were killed by Ancio and his fanatic followers. . . Today, Purano is
past marrying age, yet has not found a maiden suitable as a bride."

Elicia, though she wasn't an Indian, must have
been considered of a very high station by Purano
and his father. Things had happened here in my
absence and I had to admit that I felt a pang of
jealousy, knowing that what had happened was a
meeting of minds—and perhaps of soul—between
Elicia and Purano. Ah, the fickleness of the adolescent mind. But the jealousy was short-lived and
slightly diluted. I had been worried about how the
matter with Elicia would be resolved. Even though
I retained strong feelings for her, I knew that these
new developments were for the best. Taking Elicia
out of her jungle home, no matter how primitive,
rough and dangerous the life, would have been a
travesty. She might be as fickle as an American
high school girl, but the similarity ended there.

I took another hour's rest, during which time
Elicia still tended me with the cold, wet cloth, but
avoided my eyes as much as possible. Even when
our eyes met, I saw a kind of troubled expression in
them. She was jilting me for another man, after
having pursued me so diligently before Purano
came into her life. Finally, I decided to put her
troubled mind at ease.

"You're very beautiful and very precious,

Elicia," I said, "and I have a great fondness for you. But this is better. Purano will. . ."

"You presume too much, Senor Carter," she said. "I have announced no decisions of my intentions."

"Yes, you have," I replied. "Not with your lips, but with your eyes. Perhaps you don't love Purano yet, but you will. Don't fight it, Elicia, and don't be concerned about offending me. Let what will be come to you, naturally, and welcome it."

"You still presume. I love *you*, Senor Carter."

"And you will love Purano."

She was silent, then her eyes found mine and they were still troubled. I hadn't helped a bit.

"That is my problem," she said. "I love you both."

I nodded. I started to tell her about the vast differences in our cultures, about the fact that I would soon be called away on another assignment, perhaps halfway around the world, about the fact that I might never return to Nicarxa. I decided to skip all that malarkey. If I really wanted her, I could resign from AXE and stay right here for the rest of my life. It would be a fine surrogate for that truck farm in Ohio. Better, in fact, I said nothing, only nodded again and slipped into a deep sleep.

Before I went under, I felt the cold cloth on my forehead again, felt warm tears fall against my bare chest.

Antonio and Purano wakened me shortly before dawn. We had just over twelve hours to stop Don Carlos and his bloody revolution. If we didn't find the entrance to the cave, and if the cave didn't have a chimney that we could scale to the summit of

Alto Arete, it was all over. Even I would have difficulty escaping Nicarxa with my skin intact. And if we reached the summit, there was still the lack of a plan as to how we would function up there.

Beside me on the floor of the hut was my knapsack and I knew that the old chief had sent someone to retrieve it from the high ledge above the Reina Valley. I wished I had told him about my radio, hidden near the Cortez farm, but the radio was no help now—now that I could expect no further help from Washington. Hawk and the President drove hard bargains.

But the knapsack was a godsend. I had an extra pair of boots in there. We had all studied the map I had made of Alto Arete's layout and fortifications. Even considering that Sergeant Pequeno had lied a bit, we had a pretty fair idea of what to expect. We wouldn't have to worry about the minefields and rabid dogs and guards on the perimeter of the summit, but there were plenty of armed guards inside the compound around the main courtyard and in the palace where Don Carlos Italla lived. Unfortunately, the Marine sergeant I had killed so many days ago knew nothing of the chimney through the mountain, so there was no way of knowing where it came out on top—or if we would be able to get through it.

We were as ready, though, as we would ever be.

My fever had broken and I felt strong again. Elicia remained asleep and I was grateful for that. I didn't want to see her troubled look as her soul fought to decide between me and Purano. If the chief's son knew of her agonizing decision, he said nothing.

Outside, a dozen warriors, all carrying primitive

spears, waited for us to lead them to the cave. Botussin himself slept through our departure and, by first real light, we were well out on the trail, climbing steadily up the western slopes of Mount Toro. We walked slowly but purposefully, knowing that precious minutes were slipping past; also knowing that haste would spend our strength and make us useless once we found the cave—if we found it. It would take all the strength we could summon to scale that chimney, if indeed we could scale it at all.

Antonio carried the ancient map, studying it every few hundred yards. As we approached the first hollow that could possibly lead to the cave's hidden entrance, I thought I heard sounds ahead of us. They weren't normal jungle sounds, so I halted our small party and went on ahead to find out what the sounds were.

And there, at the mouth of the hollow, were two dozen guerillas, just rousing themselves for breakfast, in a small camp of a man-made clearing. They had been camping in the open—no tents, huts or even cots. I knew that Don Carlos had dispatched them all along this area. He knew the location of the cave and was protecting it, just in case we stumbled onto it. Because of this protection, I had the feeling that old Don Carlos considered himself safe from invasion through the lost cave. That was good. If he felt really safe, he wouldn't bother to have the top part of the chimney guarded.

I reported back to the others and we decided against a frontal attack against the superior force of guerillas. I had noticed sentries at a half-dozen outposts. We set out, knives in hands, with instructions from me on how to take out a man quietly, without alarming the others.

After staking out the sentry I would kill, I watched his activities until I found the place where he came nearest the jungle wall. I made a circuitous route to that spot, lay in the bushes and waited for the others to do the same with their sentries. Only five of the spearchuckers and I were involved in the caper. Antonio, Purano and the other seven Ninca warriors were set up in a phalanx formation near the camp's main entrance. They would press to the attack on the main force of guerillas only if one of the sentries managed to set off an alarm.

The backup phase of the operation wasn't necessary. No sooner had I leaped from cover, slashed the throat of my appointed sentry and dragged him into the brush, than the other five warriors, armed with long, keenly-honed blades, were already on top of their sentries, dispatching them silently and swiftly.

When we had dragged them all into the brush, the camp was as quiet as if nothing had happened. The balance of the guerilla force, eighteen of them, were huddled in a patch of shade near the back part of the clearing, in a narrow part of the hollow. Once again, silence and swiftness were called for. If any of the guerillas called out or escaped, they could bring reinforcements from the adjacent hollow, not more than a half mile away.

My heart really wasn't into this obvious massacre, especially since we had no idea if this were the hollow that would lead us to the ancient cave. The hieroglyphics on the map, according to Antonio, indicated that one of the seven hollows on this side of the mountain led to the cave. If the cave were at number seven and there were twenty four guerillas guarding each hollow, we would spend the entire precious day trying to kill nearly a hundred and seventy men in groups of two dozen each.

The odds in favor of us succeeding in killing all 170 men without running into a fatal snag somewhere along the line were so scant that I knew we were flirting with disaster, as well as the clock. I signaled for a council of war and we met far down the hollow beside a meandering stream.

After I had put forth my reservations and doubts, and my aversion to such a wholesale bloodbath in the seven hollows, it was agreed that we must devise an alternate plan. I turned to the taciturn Purano.

"Do you or your men know of any other trail up the mountain, one that circles around these hollows and comes out at the headwaters, nearer the base of Alto Arete?"

He studied the question, then spoke tersely with his spearchuckers. I didn't understand the language, but there was a great deal of grunting and nodding. Finally, Purano stood and gazed up the hill to the right of the first hollow.

"Come. We try old trail."

We found an old and nearly closed trail that hadn't been used in so many years that it was little better than cutting our way through the thickest part of the jungle. And it was steep, much steeper than the trail up the center of the hollow. When we had gone two hours, two very precious hours, the trail seemed to open up a bit. We moved more easily, but it was late in the morning by the time we had finished a complete survey of that side of the mountain's base.

If there were indeed a cave at the base of Alto Arete, we failed to find a trace of it. The answer lay in the fact that it must be farther down the hill, in one of the seven hollows guarded by Don Carlos Italla's guerillas. It would take too long to go back and instigate our original plan, too long even to check out the valleys from the upper end and thus circumvent the guards.

We were defeated and we all knew it as we started back down the old trail that had brought us here. Even the spearchuckers walked with a sullen gait as we started back down the mountain. My mind raced with thoughts and ideas, none of them worth a damn. Somewhere in my memory, though, was a key to all this. Someone, somewhere had said something to me to indicate that someone other than Ancio, now known as Don Carlos, knew how to decipher those damned hieroglyphics. But who? And where had I met him? Or had I merely overheard it or read of it? As we trudged along, disconsolate, not only were our spirits at low ebb, our vigilance was non-existence.

We had no idea that danger lurked until one of the Ninca spearchuckers, heading our small procession and walking far out ahead of Purano, suddenly fell in his tracks. Purano might have been silent, but he made up for it in swiftness. Even before the man was flat on the ground, Purano was off in the bushes.

The rest of us scattered, plunging into the wall of jungle on either side of the scant trail. I had my luger in my hand and lay still in the bushes, studying the trail below. I could see the Indian lying on his back, a huge throwing knife protruding from his chest.

We waited, patient, expecting an all-out attack, not even knowing who our attackers might be. In the stillness, we heard someone move in the brush far down the trail. A man in peasant garb and carrying a rifle over his shoulder, stepped into the trail and walked boldly up to the dead spearchucker. He looked around, saw nothing threatening, then bent to pull his knife out of the Indian's chest.

A spear came flying from out of the jungle and caught the man in the throat. He fell back, clutching his wound and the spear with both hands. His eyes bulged and he kept coughing like a consumptive. Soon, though, he gave up the struggle and fell across the body of the dead Indian.

The jungle was quiet again. I waited perhaps five minutes, then went down to check the dead bodies. I turned the peasant over and saw that he was one of the guerillas we had seen in the camp at the mouth of the first hollow. Danger bells jangled all through my head. The others were coming out of their hiding places, but I waved them back and plunged once again into the jungle. Not a moment too soon. I had just turned to peer back at the trail when I saw six more guerillas, their automatic rifles at the ready, creep up the trail. They stopped when they saw the two dead men and I knew they were about to open fire on the surrounding jungle. I opened my mouth and let out a single word, loud, raucous and anxious:

"Attack."

Antonio and I opened fire at the same time. A split second behind us, Purano and his spearchuckers let go their lethal weapons. Purano himself leaped into the trail and started after the guerillas, knife in hand. Antonio and I stopped firing, to avoid hitting him.

The remaining guerillas, seeing the tall, strong apparition coming down on them with teeth bared and knife flashing, took off running. A new volley of spears sailed accurately past Purano and found marks on the backs of the fleeing guerillas.

Only one of them remained alive, none got away. It wasn't necessary to torture the poor devil to get information. He looked around at his massacred friends and talked as willingly and as profusely as that Cuban Marine sergeant had talked back there in the Cortez stable the night I had literally strung him up by his balls.

He said guerillas at the mouth of the first hollow had quickly missed their sentries. Rather than send for help from an adjacent hollow, they had split up in squads and had set out to find out what had happened to their sentries. This squad had been searching for two hours, finally locating this old trail but not expecting to find anyone. One of the guerillas had run on ahead. He was the one who had spotted the Indian and had killed him by throwing his knife at him. The others hadn't known what was happening up ahead and had walked into our trap.

By now, the guerilla said, the other search teams had probably sought help from others. The hill would soon be swarming with search teams, leaving the valleys unguarded. It seemed to be our grand opportunity to search for the ancient cave. But I looked at my watch and saw that it was well past noon. In about eight hours, it would be dusk and Don Carlos would send up the signal from the top of Alto Arete.

The guerilla, of course, had no idea where the cave entrance was. He had merely been given orders not to let anyone pass up the hollow; he wasn't even to go up the hollow himself. That was why the search teams had gone up the ridge, and had unhappily stumbled onto us.

After conferring with Purano and Antonio, I

found the future prospects dimmer than I'd previously thought. It would take at least an hour to check out each of the seven hollows. Unless we hit the cave on our first two or three tries, it would be too late to stop Don Carlos. Even after we found the cave, Purano pointed out as succinctly as possible, it would take many hours to scale the natural chimney. It was, after all, more than two thousand feet long.

For the first time in many years, it looked rather conclusively that Nick Carter, N3, Killmaster for AXE, would fail in an assignment. Not only fail, but be lucky to get out of it alive.

But there was an answer somewhere in my mind, something that could shorten the time considerably, enable us to find the cave in a matter of an hour or two, giving us ample time to scale the chimney and reach Don Carlos Italla's lair in the clouds.

But what was the answer, and who had it?

We dragged all the dead bodies off the trail and, with the sole surviving guerilla securely tied, we started off down the trail again. This time, we moved with more caution, keeping our eyes and ears peeled for the search teams. It wasn't likely they'd all cover the same ground, but with our luck one team could get lost and accidentally stumble across our path. It was a possibility we couldn't overlook.

We were near the mouth of the hollow when Purano suddenly stopped and held up his hand. We all took to the brush, weapons ready. We could all hear it then. Someone was thrashing his way up the hill, ignoring stealth, coming hell bent for election.

I crouched in the brush, my hand gripped tightly

around Wilhelmina's butt. The thrashing became louder and it sounded as though a whole troop of Marines was making its way up the faint trail, knocking aside trees, vines and brush, kicking fallen logs.

I saw a flash of cloth and raised the luger. I was sighting down the barrel, tightening my finger on the trigger, ready to fire as soon as I had a clear shot at the target. I would get the first in line and let the others concentrate on those behind.

I had just about reached the point of no return on Wilhelmina's trigger when I saw who was coming. I damned near threw the luger away then.

In another fraction of a second, I would have killed Elicia Cortez.

She was alone and in a hurry. She had forgotten all I'd taught her about traveling in the jungle when there were enemy troops about. She had been in such a hurry to find us, to be with us, she had ignored danger. And she had almost paid for that ignoring with her life. I was trembling when I came out of the brush and saw her still plunging up the trail.

"Senor Carter," she cried. "Oh, Nick, I thought you were dead. I thought you were all dead."

She was crying as she lunged into my arms and began to shower my face, grizzly now with several days' growth of beard, with sweet, wet kisses. I held her loosely and glanced back over my shoulder at Purano, who had been smiling at her arrival. He was now scowling at us both. Jealousy. It can work wonders, even among the best of allies.

Elicia saw him, too, but her response was quite different. She leaped back out of my arms and suddenly turned darker in a blush. She glanced at Purano's eyes, then her eyes fell and she looked at the ground near his feet.

"I was fearful for you as well," she said. "It gives me pleasure to see you healthy and well."

That was all the mush stuff Purano needed. His eyes gazed at the ground near Elicia's feet and he made the longest speech of his brief life.

"It gives me pleasure that you are pleased that I am well. I fear for you, also, and am delighted to find you healthy and well."

I stood back and watched Elicia Cortez turn into a rose in that moment, budding, blossoming, flowering—more than Purano knew.

I had to break up the unusual courtship, though.

"Why did you come looking for us, Elicia?"

She tore her eyes away from the ground near Purano's feet and looked at me, steadily, without her usual shyness. "The hermit came to the Indian camp to warn Botussin," she said. "The Iman from Apalca has given his assent to a revolution in both Nicarxa and Apalca. The revolution is to begin at nightfall. No one else knows that agreement has been reached. Once the signal has been given from Alto Arete, a special contingent of guerillas, part of Don Carlos Italla's elite corps, is to attack the Ninca lands and kill every man, woman and child."

"How does Pico know all this?" By then, Antonio and the others had formed a circle around us, all listening with keen ears and wide eyes.

"He has a radio," Elicia said. "He took it with him when he went to the mountain to live away from man. He makes periodic trips to the capital, disguised as a monk, to buy parts and batteries. He has been listening to frequencies he has learned about in his listening. He has heard coded communications between Don Carlos and the Cubans.

With so much time on his hand, old Pico has broken the code."

A thought came. "I've been told that Don Carlos will signal the beginning of the revolution with a flare gun from the top of Alto Arete. If he has sophisticated radio equipment, why doesn't he spread the word that way?"

"I can answer that," Antonio said. "We are still a poor country, Senor Carter. Not many people have radios. Not even Don Carlos has been able to equip all his revolutionary groups throughout the island with radio equipment. But a flare at dusk from Alto Arete can be seen from every point on the island, even in Apalca and far out at sea. Even, it is said, in Cuba."

Good God, I thought. That flare has more significance than I had imagined. Somehow, I had to stop Don Carlos from shooting off that flare. Without it, he might radio a few of his contingents —the Cubans mostly—but not enough to make the revolution a total success. But how?

I thought of old Pico sitting up there on his hidden plateau listening to all of Don Carlos Italla's radio communications. This man, who had sought a place away from the company of men. I recalled the sadness in his voice when he had told me about what had happened to his beautiful eleven-year-old daughter:

I could tell by his eyes that he was lying. That was when I followed him and his friends and learned that he had indeed lied, and I came away a broken man.

Thoughts began to tumble through my brain. I thought my head would explode trying to sort them out. They were a jumble of thoughts, leading everywhere and nowhere. In that jumble of thoughts was the answer I had been seeking. I grabbed Elicia by her slender arms.

"Elicia, where is the hermit now? Where is Pico?"

"With Chief Botussin. He will stay there and help fight the elite corps when they come to murder the Nincas."

"Does he know where we are, what we're trying to do?"

"I don't know. I only know what he told the chief. After that, they sat down to a big dinner, planning to discuss strategy later."

It figured. Botussin's stomach came before everything. Pico didn't know that we were looking for the cave entrance. If he did. . .

"Let's go," I said to Antonio and Purano. "Elicia, you stay with the others and come back to the Ninca camp. We'll go on ahead. I have to talk with Pico."

"Why. . ."

"Just do as I say. There isn't a minute to lose."

As Antonio, Purano and I hurried down the trail, heading for the tribe's camp, I explained what I hoped to learn from Pico.

Perhaps the old hermit couldn't remember a day thirty years ago when he had followed Ancio and his evil friends to a cave at the base of Alto Arete, in one of seven hollows.

But there were other memories, other knowledges, that hadn't been concealed deep in his mind by tragedies. Remembering the one might open the door to the other.

If I could tap those other memories, those other knowledges, there was a slim chance of saving the people of these two island countries.

If not?

I wouldn't think of that just yet.

CHAPTER SEVEN

My second meeting with Pico, the hermit, was a mixture of pleasures and disappointments. Or, as the comedians like to remind us somewhat monotonously, some good news and some bad news.

First off, he was angry at me for having left his camp on my own.

"I spent years, Senor Carter," he said, crouching among the short Indians to diminish the effect of his great height, "concealing the trail to my hermitage. No living man but you knows now how to come there. Besides, you weren't ready to leave. The poultice needed several more hours to do its work."

We were in the square of the tribal encampment. The hot midday sun blazed down on the mixture of white and brown bodies. Flies the size of teacups buzzed around us. Some of them even attacked the bandages on my side and my right foot. Shooing them away was a dangerous activity, fraught with promise of reprisal.

Antonio and Purano flanked the fat chief on one side of the circle. A little behind them were Elicia and the spearchuckers from the mission to the seven hollows. The body of the dead spearchucker was in a special burial hut, being prepared by the few remaining women of the tribe. I sat beside Pico on the other side of the circle. Filling in the circle, on either side of the hermit and I, were the village elders I had seen that first night in the council hut. Other spearchuckers, jealous that they hadn't gone on the mission to share in the glory, surrounded all of us, a circle outside a circle.

"The poultice did its work well," I assured Pico. "If it had done much better, it would be like not having had a wound at all. But I do apologize for breaking your rule. Will you accept?"

Pico grinned. It was all the acceptance I would receive. "You must promise never to tell another living soul how you left my camp."

"I won't." Actually, I couldn't. It had been darker than the inside of a pig the night I had left his camp. If I were given the chore of finding my way back there, I would probably wander in the jungle for the rest of my life.

"Now, what is it you wish of me, Senor Carter?" he asked after the amenities and the chastizing were over. "What is the purpose of such hurrying back here to talk to me?"

I refreshed his memory about our conversation, about his saying that he had followed Ancio and his friends, had learned that the man had indeed lied, and had seen his daughter and several others covered with oil and burned. I repeated as much as I could remember of what he had said, hoping to spark memories from him. Important memories.

"I want to know everything you saw and heard that night," I told Pico. "I know it's painful remembering, but this is important. I want to know as much as you can possibly remember before I show you something of great importance."

He looked puzzled. So did all the others. But everyone remained silent while Pico considered the request. I was conscious of the minutes ticking away, of the day and the mission being completely shattered, while this old hermit searched back through thirty years of memories.

"I was there, as I have told you," he said, his voice sounding deep and hollow, his eyes starting to mist. "I remember so little, no more than what I told you. I saw the cave. I saw the seashell necklace that I had made for my daughter. It was on the body of a naked corpse. That is how I was able to tell that it was her."

His voice cracked then and I wanted him to stop that particular line of thought. It wasn't necessary to recall details of the inside of the cave, of the grisly scene there. I wanted him to recall details of the outside, of how to get there. But I knew enough about idea association to let him ramble in his own way, as time slipped past, minute by minute.

But he was finished with his grim recollections. He looked at me blankly, puzzled over what I was seeking. I didn't want to lead him. It was important that his mind be free of prejudice when he saw what I had to show him.

"Do you recall any details of when you followed Ancio and his friends into the mountains?" I asked.

He spent some time thinking. Precious time. My anxiety grew.

"I was under great stress at the time," he said. "I had anticipated that my daughter was gone, but I had no idea. . ." He stopped, swept the circle of interested faces with deeply sad eyes, and said, "it was thirty years ago. I recall many scenes quite well. They are emblazoned on my soul. However. . ."

That was the worst of the bad news. He had no idea whatsoever of where the cave entrance was. I wouldn't be able to jog his memory with further questions, and I was afraid of even more bad news when I sprang my one and only possibility. But there was no more time to waste. I turned to Antonio.

"Would you get the map and show it to Pico."

"The map?" Antonio asked, puzzled. "Senor Carter, it is in Indian hieroglyphics and, if the Indians can't read the symbols, how can you expect. . ."

"Pico was a professor of anthropology at Nicarxa University," I said, looking at Pico to confirm that my memory of what he had told me that day at his hermitage was correct. "He was head of the department of Indian Culture when he became involved in a revolutionary activity that changed his life forever. Am I correct, Pico, in assuming that, as head of the department of Indian Culture, you would have been required to learn the various hieroglyphics used by all the tribes in this area?"

Pico nodded. "You have a map? What kind of map?"

I asked Chief Botussin to explain about the map. It was a mistake. The old chief wound himself up a tangled web of words that seemed to have no end-ing. It took five precious minutes for him to reach his point: that the map showed Ancio how to find the cave entrance and that his warriors took the map from Ancio and that it had been kept in a secret hiding place ever since and that he would be sorely tried if it fell into evil hands, etcetera.

"May I see it?" Pico asked.

Antonio had the map in a leather pouch strapped to the small of his back. He quickly undid the pouch and handed the fragile parchment over to Pico. The old man studied it for more time than I would have liked him to spend on it. The sun got hotter, the flies meaner and the day much, much shorter. Pico finally looked up and saw the worried looks on all our faces. He grinned at me.

"Don't worry so much about the time, Senor Carter," he said. "I have good news about that. The signal will not be given before sundown. At this time of year, sundown will come shortly after 8:30. You have ample time."

I looked at my watch, a digital creation that was a gift from David Hawk. It was full of lifetime batteries. And the numbers read 12:22. I breathed a small sigh of relief. I had estimated that we had perhaps six or seven hours to stop Don Carlos from sending the signal. We actually had more than eight hours. Yet, it was no great solace learning that piece of good news—we could use, I was sure, more than eight *days* and still be cutting it close.

"The big concern is the map," I said, "and whether you can read the hieroglyphics. Can you?"

"Oh yes. In my time on the mountainside, I had many hours to continue my studies. And I took along textbooks from anthropologists and socio-

logists who have recorded the hieroglyphics of all
the ancient tribes in Central and South America. I
knew them by heart when I was actively teaching,
but I could have forgotten them in thirty years, as
I forgot the trail to the cave. Fortunately, I loved
my work as a professor of anthropology, so I kept
up. However. . ."

We all sucked in breath, anticipating another
round of bad news. We got it.

"The critical area of the map is far too faint to be
seen, even by the best of eyes. The map shows a
trail leading from an ancient encampment over
there—" he raised a long arm and pointed off to
the west—"to a point near the mouths of seven valleys." He pointed to the northeast. "But that section concerning the hollows and the cave itself are
so faded that—I'm sorry, but it's hopeless."

Bad news—in spades. He could read the map,
but seeing it hadn't lifted the veil that covered his
memory, hadn't triggered any sharp or even faint
details of the route to the cave entrance. And a vital part of the map was too faded to be read.

"What I don't understand," I said, "is how Ancio—or Don Carlos—was able to use this map to
find the cave entrance."

"It was easy for him," Pico said. "As Chief
Botussin said, he was coached by the old man who
entrusted the map to him. And there's another
thing. This fading is a recent thing, brought on by
Ancio's careless handling of the map. Then, again,
the man had all the time in the world to find that
cave, while our time, you must admit, is sorely lim-
ited."

There was a deep silence in the twin circles in the
hot sun and the square of the Ninca village. Old

Pico looked from face to face, then returned to a study of the map. More minutes passed. My watch read out at 12:36. *Less* than eight hours to go. If we had the answer this very minute, I calculated, it would take us two hours to get to the cave entrance, depending on which hollow it was in. That would give us six hours to make what had been calculated as a four-hour climb. We had, then, two hours to spare, two hours in which to learn the mystery of the map.

It was obvious to all of us that we wouldn't be able to make out that damned map in two hours, two days, or even two years. Perhaps even two lifetimes. Fat old Botussin began to shift nervously on the stool his buttocks had swallowed up on the ground. He was anxious to end this fruitless confab and set up his defenses against Don Carlos Italla's elite corps. We could expect them just minutes after the 8:30 signal was given. I knew the old chief was considering moving the Indian village back to the ancient site shown on the map. That would give the Nincas more time, but we all knew that the elite corps would soon find that location. In a matter of days, perhaps even hours.

By tomorrow at this time, there would be no more Ninca Indians in the country of Nicarxa. And, unless another miracle occurred, no more Nick Carter. After my killing of Col. Ramon Vasco, I could count on the fact that my name was high on the list of kills, probably higher than the names of the Nincas.

Pico stirred on the ground, held the map up toward the sun to look at it from a new angle. We waited for Botussin to call an end to the meeting, to start preparing his final defenses. The chief opened his mouth to speak, but Pico held up his enormous hand for silence. He had a new thought. Good news or bad news?

"High above my plateau," he said, more to himself than to the rest of us, "there is a certain herb I found that I boiled into a clear liquid. I coated the print on some of my books, print that was growing faint. Or perhaps it was only my eyes going faint. In any event, the print grew darker, more distinct. I could read it more easily."

He paused again and we were all up on our toes, waiting for him to go on. Even old Botussin was leaning forward so far that I expected to hear the invisible legs of his stool snap like matchsticks. He wouldn't have much of a fall, his overflowing buttocks were almost touching the ground as it was. Behind me, Elicia had sucked in her breath and was holding it. I wondered if her brown skin would turn blue if the old hermit didn't continue talking soon.

"Of course," Pico went on, "the liquid used on my books might destroy this old parchment altogether, or it may not work at all. In my opinion, it is worth a try."

It was good news, or potentially good news.

"How long will it take?" I asked, still clock-conscious.

Pico shrugged. "Miracles must not be shackled to the schedules of man," he said. "It will take however long it takes. I will return when the task is done. If it is successful, I will return to help find the entrance to the cave. If it is not, I will return to help defend against the elite corps."

He got up and started off alone. I knew that the elite corps was already taking up positions in the region, in anticipation of Don Carlos Italla's flare signal. I also knew that the guerillas guarding the mouths of the seven hollows would still be out searching for those who had killed so many of their number.

"Some of us will go with you, Pico," I said, stopping the hermit. "Your journey is perhaps the most important ever taken in this country. We can't have you ambushed and killed on the trail."

"I will accept an escort to a certain point," Pico said, grinning again to show that he wasn't ready yet to let others know of his hidden plateau. "But you must remain here, Senor Carter."

"Oh, no you. . ."

"That is a condition," Pico said curtly. "If you are to lead the climb up the chimney, if we find the cave, you will need all the strength you possess. You have pushed yourself too much already. If you don't stay and rest, I will not even try to clarify the mysteries of this old map."

A part of me accepted what he said; that part of me wanted to rest, to let the tensions and the fatigue drain away. Another part, the part that has made me the top Killmaster for AXE, wanted to continue to push, to be in on the action, all the action. The first part won.

I watched from the edge of the square as the giant hermit went down the trail. He was flanked by Antonio and Purano. Behind them went two dozen warriors, spears in hand. I kept my weapons just in case the guerillas from the hollows found their way into the Ninca camp.

Chief Botussin arose from his stool and I was surprised to find that it hadn't been damaged, that the legs hadn't been punched into the ground.

"You sleep," he said, pointing to the council hut. "My servants will clear out the flies and put shades over the windows and door to provide quiet dark for your slumber. Don't expect the hermit for at least two hours. Sleep well."

Some order that. If it took Pico two hours to return with the solution, that left only six hours. The climb up the chimney would take four hours, at least, but there was a two-hour journey to the seven hollows. We had no slack time at all. With such troubled thoughts, I lay on the pallet in the darkened council hut to try to sleep. Elicia, I presumed, had gone off to stay with the tribal women until Pico's return. I hadn't seen her when I had turned back from watching Pico, Antonio, Purano and the warriors disappear down the trail.

I lay there and felt the hopelessness, the desolation, of our plight settle down over my mind. It was hopeless, and I knew it. That parchment was two hundred years old and the ink used to make those symbols had no relationship whatever to the inks used in Pico's books. The herbs he found above the plateau wouldn't have the same effect on the parchment that it had on the books. But I was willing to go along because the experiment spelled hope for these people. If they were to die in a matter of hours—days at the most—let them retain hope as long as possible. The death of hope has always signalled the death of the cause. But hope, I was convinced, was all that we had to go on now.

The good news, I was certain, wasn't really good news at all. It was a vision in the jungle, an ephemeral presence like an image projected on a wall of fog. With that unhappy thought, I began to drift into sleep.

A soft, pleasant dream was already starting. I was in the George Cinq Hotel dining room in Paris. Across from me was Diane Northrup, a woman I had loved in an earlier time. She was smiling, sipping from a glass of champagne. The orchestra was playing our favorite song. Diane leaned forward to kiss me and I heard a familiar voice, close by, sweet, bell-like and melodic:

"When my love is near me,
I am like the rose;
Budding, flowering, blossoming,
More than my love knows."

Still half asleep, I couldn't believe that I would mix Diane Northrup and Elicia Cortez in the same dream. I couldn't imagine Elicia in the dining room of the very proper George Cinq Hotel in Paris, anymore than I could imagine Diane here in this hot hut in the middle of an Indian village in the Caribbean.

Something soft crept up along my chest. Something even softer, and smelling of orange blossoms, pressed against my shoulder. And then naked legs touched mine, slipped up over me and began to move gently back and forth.

I came fully awake, out of a pleasant dream into a far more pleasant reality.

Elicia was beside me on the pallet. She was naked and her hair was still damp from having bathed in the stream below the village. Once again, she had found orange blossoms and had crushed them against her skin, from head to toe.

I gazed into her loving eyes and still couldn't convince myself that I wasn't dreaming. She kissed my lips and I found my arm going around her back, caressing the soft, sweet-smelling skin. My hand went down to her gently-rising buttocks and I felt the erection building magnificently at my middle. This was no dream.

"Elicia, do you know what you're doing?"

She shushed me with a fragrant finger across my lips. "I know," she said. "No talk. Only love."

All right, I had tried. Time and again, I had turned away from the pleasures that this girl had offered me. Time and again, I had felt noble about my intentions, about my abstinence. Well, there is a time to put all that jazz behind you. That time was now.

Days of frustration and abstinence and temptation had built up a tremendous drive inside me. My erection was more than an erection. It was a budding, blossoming, flowering instrument of sex and love and lust and frustration. Elicia found the hardness and enclosed it with her hand.

There were no more thoughts about what would happen to Elicia when this caper was over. There were no more thoughts about whether she belonged to me or to Purano. There were no more concerns for whether she was still a virgin by the flesh or by the soul. The future had no place in my mind. Or my body. The needs of the flesh and of the soul were so intense, so ready, for each of us that we shut out past and future and plunged helter-skelter into the present.

I started gently, recalling the brutal rapings this girl had endured for three months from the Cuban Marines. She seemed to like it. I raised up and gazed at those erect, ripe breasts that had tantalized me so often in her loose blouse. I kissed the nipples, tenderly, then with more purpose. I sucked and she arched her back and raised her pubis to me. I lay my hardness along the mound and gently massaged until she let out a moan and bit my ear.

"Enough gentleness," she said, gasping, chewing on my ear. "Take me now and let me know the pleasure of losing my virginity to one I love. Oh, Nick, love me for now, for now only."

When I entered her, she was ready. She climaxed almost instantly and I thought it was over. She took a few seconds of respite and then the passion grew in her to a newer and higher level. She swallowed me up, rising and falling, plunging and withdrawing. She climaxed three more times before it finally happened to me. I had been holding back, savoring it, wanting it to go on forever—or, at least, for the next two hours. But nothing lasts forever. She responded by climaxing again, for the fifth time. I have always envied women that capacity, but I wouldn't have traded that one gigantic climax for all the little ones in the world.

Spent, sated, we lay sweating on the pallet. Elicia's arm lay across my now naked chest. She was silent for such a long time that I thought she was asleep. She wasn't.

"You will think me strange," she finally said, "but I did this as a gesture of farewell."

"Farewell?"

"Yes. In two weeks, I will marry Purano and join his tribe. I told him about you, about how I feel, about how I will always feel about you. He knows that I am with you now."

"He knows? And he agreed to this?"

"Yes, otherwise, he would know that I would always wonder what it would have been like. You see, Nick, I know nothing of love. I mean, this kind of love. What happened to me with those Marines was a world apart from what happened here today. I knew it would be so. Purano understands. Unless I could prove to myself that this beautiful act could be truly beautiful, I would not be a fit bride. Do you understand that?"

I have been all over this globe and have met and been exposed to the cultures of hundreds of peoples. I have undestood much. I had to admit, though, that I didn't fully understand this weird triangle between me, Purano and Elicia, or why he would agree to have her come to me when they had just become betrothed. It was equally difficult to comprehend when I knew that Purano had remained single because there were so few suitable maidens in the tribe. There were so few maidens because thirty years ago the surviving females had been "spoiled" by Ancio and his gang. I understood a part of it, then. Spoiled had different meanings. Ancio had taken the maidens against their will, therefore spoiling them. Elicia and I had engaged in an activity of mutual agreement, as, I'm sure, Purano and Elicia would do before their marriage. But that was cutting the culture pretty thin and I didn't understand it at all.

"I understand," I lied.

"Good. It is important for me and Purano that you do."

We slept then, but only for fifteen or twenty minutes. I awoke first and was trying to understand more fully why this girl felt she had to give herself to me before her marriage to Purano, to make it a farewell gesture even though she confessed that she loved me every bit as much as she loved Purano. I couldn't understand. What happened next was even more difficult to understand.

Elicia awoke, came to me and we made love again. This second time, she said, would prepare her for a lifetime of joy in the man she had chosen to marry. I didn't try to understand that one either. I merely enjoyed, even though there was a growing sadness that this would be the last of Elicia for me.

There was shouting out in the square and we quickly dressed. Elicia walked boldly out the front door and I followed, a sheepish grin on my face. If the others in the square knew about our tryst, about Elicia's strange logic on how to say farewell to the man she was turning down, they gave no hint of it.

The shouting was because a sentry below had spotted Pico, Antonio, Purano and the warriors returning. I checked my watch. They'd been gone just over an hour. We were well within the schedule, if Pico had anything to offer concerning the map and the hidden cave.

He had.

The circles formed again in the square, with Pico and the map at the center. Behind Chief Botussin, I noticed, Elicia had moved up beside Purano and they were conversing in that strange ritual of staring at the ground near each other's feet. She was probably telling him about our love-making. With a slightly bitter thought, I figured she was telling him that I was a lousy lover, that he had nothing to worry about. But no, I thought again, she would be truthful. The truth was that we both were good lovers. Purano would have to go some to replace my performance in Elicia's eyes. I wondered, with another ping of jealousy, if she would sing the rose song to him. I knew she would.

"Time was saved," Pico said, "because I still had

a supply of the clear liquid from my last batch. I had to coat the parchment three times, but the third time the images became distinct. As you can see, the cave is near the top of the fifth hollow from the east, or the third hollow from the west. It would have taken several hours to search all the hollows. Worse yet, without the map, we would not have found the cave even if we had gone directly to the fifth hollow."

He pointed to a faded mark that looked like a child's rendering of a fly. They were big on flies in this part of the world.

"The fly once was the symbol of fertility among the Nincas," Pico continued. It still was judging from the size of the flies that were right now munching on me. "This fly is facing due west, indicating that the cave entrance is to the west side of the hollow. Possibly, there's a ravine there separating hollow five from hollow six. We won't know until we inspect the premises. But I've found a small dot that I don't understand. Under the magnifying glass, the dot is actually a tiny circle. Whether this was by intent or by accident, I don't know. If by accident, it means nothing. If by design, it means that the cave entrance is through a well or a deep hole in the ground. Finding a hole up there will be like looking for the proverbial needle in a haystack. I know that I followed Ancio and his friends down some steps in a dark place. The open circle on the map indicates the presence of water, but I recall no water. My memory is of no help to us. And there's more potential bad news."

We waited. Pico gazed at the faces, then glanced at the sun that was telling that it was mid-afternoon. I checked my watch. It was 2:26. We were tight on time, but there was enough if we had no further problems.

"When we were returning from my plateau," Pico said, "we saw a group of red-shirted guerillas moving up toward the area of the hollows. These are the elite corps of Don Carlos, of Ancio. There were perhaps a hundred of them. If we encounter them on the trail, it is all over.

"Then," I said as positively as I could, "we'll just not encounter them. Unless you have anything to add, Pico, I think we ought to leave immediately for the cave entrance."

After a brief altercation between Elicia and Purano about her going along, it was decided by old Chief Botussin that, if the Ninca tribe was to link up with the Twentieth Century at last, they might as well accept the new role for women. In short, he said, Purano shouldn't tell the girl what she could or couldn't do. Elicia went along and, even though Purano had nodded his approval, his face and eyes didn't seem any too happy about the decision.

I had already been keeping my eyes on Purano since spending that lovely hour alone in the council hut with Elicia. The boy had known that Elicia was in love with me, had been with me on the trail. But it had seemed to me a somewhat extreme test of his love to tell him, as Elicia had, that she was going to give herself to another man before the marriage. The more I thought of it, the more I realized that women in other cultures were similar in that respect. A great number of American women have a final fling with a former lover before entering into marriage. The difference, though, is they keep quiet about it.

So far, I hadn't seen any signs of animosity out of Purano. He treated me with his usual silent respect. If he was plotting any mischief against me out of jealousy, he didn't show it. And we hadn't been on the trail ten minutes before his obvious pique about losing his first argument with Elicia seemed to have dissipated.

There were seventeen of us in the party heading out to find the entrance to the sacrifical cave and, hopefully, a way to the top of Alto Arete. Besides me, Elicia, Antonio, Purano and Pico, there were twelve warriors armed with knives and spears. We left the Indian camp at 2:32 in the afternoon, giving us just six hours to reach Don Carlos Italla's lair and to stop him from giving the war signal.

We had no time for toe-stubbing.

Purano and his warriors led our party. Purano knew of secret trails which would take a few minutes longer, but which would keep us out of danger from the guerilla patrols. Even so, we spotted the red-shirted members of the elite corps in half a dozen places before we even approached the entrance to the fifth hollow.

Strangely, there were no guards or guerillas at the mouth of the fifth hollow. It was quiet there; not a soul was about. We found the campfires used by guards only recently, and places on the jungle floor where they had slept. The warriors in our group spread out to make certain the guerillas weren't waiting in ambush, but the whole area was clear.

As we made our way up the hollow, through ever-narrowing ravines and along high ledges above a cascading stream, I began to feel more and more uneasy about the absence of guards. If we had spotted guerillas and avoided them, I would have felt easier. At least, we would have known where they were.

This way, the jungle hollow had an eerie feeling about it. Even the birds and the rushing water seemed to have muted sounds, as though anticipating a disaster.

As we neared the top of the hollow and were weary from an hour-long forced march over difficult trails, Pico called a halt and we rested. He sat down and studied the ancient map, getting up frequently to check certain points. Elicia and Purano sat side by side on the grass, gazing at invisible points near each other's feet. I wondered just how those two would help propagate the race among the Nincas, but decided it was none of my business.

I used the time to study my crude map of the top of Alto Arete, based on information I had gleaned from Luis Pequeno, the hapless Marine sergeant who had helped me plunge into this whole mad affair. There were squares for the main buildings; the barracks for the monks, the minefields and other fortifications. Even as I pondered the map, I had the distinct feeling that it would be useless. Luis Pequeno could have lied through his teeth about everything, or he could have made the whole thing up just to keep me from torturing him. But it was all I had to go on and I had the others study it closely.

We moved on. It was 3:45 when Pico spotted a deep ravine separating the fifth and sixth hollows. He had been right about that. We slid down the steep banks and came up on the other side, through a wall of vines and into a small clearing about the size of a high school gymnasium.

It was quiet in the clearing, quieter than it had been on the trail. Not even the sound of the tumbling water from the ravine behind us reached our ears. Not one bird sang or called out. Pico spotted a mound of rocks at the far end of the clearing, up a steep slope.

"That would be where the well is," he said. "If my calculations and faint memory are correct, the entrance will be through the well."

I had a great deal of nylon rope in my knapsack, and Purano and his warriors had brought long lengths of well-made hemp rope. We could use it all for climbing down the well—and possibly for climbing up the natural chimney. The husky Indian and Pico started off briskly up the slope. The hemp rope in hand.

For some reason I still haven't been able to fathom, I decided to remain behind. I smelled danger. I signalled Antonio to take a post to my right with his Volska automatic weapon. I pointed toward the mound of rocks and Antonio dropped to one knee. He aimed at the rocks. Elicia, unaware of our vigilance, went on up the slope with Purano, Pico and the warriors.

My hunch of danger proved true. Pico was no more than halfway across the clearing when guerillas came streaming out from either side of the rock pile. They opened fire and the big hermit was the first to fall. The warriors began to let out hideous warcries and then flung their spears.

The spears fell harmlessly against the rocks and the guerillas advanced down the slope, cutting the warriors to pieces with automatic rifles.

Antonio was going crazy near me. He wanted to

fire and I kept holding him back. Elicia had seen the guerillas and had made a dash for the jungle off to her right. She was temporarily out of danger.

"Wait, Antonio," I said, watching the guerillas murder the now unarmed Indians. "Our only chance is surprise. They don't know we're here."

I signalled for him to move up the right side of the clearing. The guerillas had stopped and were watching the warriors who were all on their bellies in the high grass. I counted six guerillas, all armed, then set off up the left side of the clearing.

As I was easing back into a clump of bushes halfway up the slope, I saw that Antonio was doing the same across from me. The guerillas were still near the top of the slope, eyeing the fallen Indians for signs of life. I felt a sick feeling at the pit of my stomach and was convinced that all twelve, plus Pico and Purano, had been killed in the withering gunfire.

Slowly, the guerillas began to edge down the slope to inspect their kill. I raised my rifle and signalled to Antonio to hold off firing. All six guerillas advanced down the slope. Just as I was considering that a stupid move and was ready to open fire, four more guerillas came rushing down from the rocks, firing madly.

If they had waited one second more, they would have caught Antonio and I in a trap.

I opened fire when all ten guerillas were together. Antonio, across the clearing, did the same. The guerilla band split, some running in all directions. Two came down the slope, firing from their hips. I picked them off cleanly, then went after three who were running back up the slope, toward the safety of the rocks.

But four of the guerillas stood their ground.

Crouching just above the fallen Indians, they singled out Antonio and began blasting away at him. I knew I was next. I ducked into the jungle wall and started upward, hoping to come out at a better vantage point. It was then that I heard Elicia scream out Antonio's name.

There was more screaming and yelling in that clearing as I struggled against the heavy vines and underbrush. I couldn't make any headway in the jungle, so I found a new opening to the clearing and went rushing through.

Four of the Indian spearchuckers were up. They were struggling with the guerillas in hand-to-hand combat. Below, I saw Antonio lying flat on his face in the grass. Elicia was dashing down the slope to him.

I looked back toward the struggling warriors and guerillas and knew that the automatic weapon was useless here. If I opened fire, I would kill friends and enemies alike. I reached back and snaked Wilhelmina from the tape.

Kneeling, I singled out a guerilla and took careful aim. The luger boomed and seemed to shake the trees around the clearing. But a guerilla went down. One by one, I picked off five guerillas and made a quick count in my head. Of ten guerillas, we had killed seven. Three were missing.

Worse yet, of the twelve Indian warriors Botussin had sent with us, eight were dead. Purano had been shot in the shoulder and Pico had slight wounds in his thigh and left arm. Both could walk, but they would never be able to climb that chimney to Alto Arete.

While Pico and Purano rallied the four surviving spearchuckers to go look for the three guerillas who had got away, I went down the slope to check on Antonio. Elicia was hovering over him, hugging his head to her bosom, crying softly. I could see from ten paces away that he was dead.

He was. His body was full of holes from the rain of bullets. I shuddered to think that, if I hadn't plunged into the forest wall when I did, my body would look much like his.

"We'll come back for him," I said gently to Elicia. "When it is over, we'll take him to the Indian camp for a proper burial."

She got up and went into the jungle. I waited, watching the minutes flip past on my digital watch. It was twenty minutes past four. We had just ten minutes to find the caves and begin our climb up that chimney.

But death has a way of stalling time, of making it stand still. I could do nothing but wait for Elicia's grief to run its course.

To make matters worse, the four warriors returned and told Purano in stilted whispers that they had lost the three guerillas they had been sent to dispatch. I calculated the distance to the nearest guerilla camp and figured we had plenty of time to be out of here before the alarm went out in any effective manner. Of course, there were the red-shirted guerillas of Don Carlos Italla's elite corps parading about and they could be here in minutes, but I decided not to let that worry me. Not much, anyway.

After five minutes, Elicia came back into the clearing, her eyes dry. In her hands was a cluster of wild roses she had found in the thicket.

She crossed her dead brother's hands over his chest and lay the roses on his hands. Then, she looked up at me.

"We will go now and kill the beast on the mountain."

The three guerillas who had escaped death in the battle in the clearning were still nowhere to be seen. Pico and I led the way to the rocks and then all of us began tossing the stones aside. Even Purano worked with his one good arm and rolled huge boulders down the slope and into the jungle.

It took ten minutes to clear away enough rocks so that we could see the top of the well. A very precious ten minutes.

The well was covered with a cut stone slab about the size of the top of a pool table. It took all of us to nudge it aside, inch by inch, until there was a big enough opening for one of us to slip inside. Pico took a small rock and dropped it into the well.

Less than a second later, we heard the splash. Pico shook his head.

"No good," he said. "The map was right, although I'm certain there was no water here thirty years ago. There must be a system for draining and filling it at will, but it would take us days to learn the key to that system. The cave entrance, the tunnel I recall crawling through after going down many steps, is filled with water. Perhaps even the cave itself is full of water."

We stood there on that pile of stones and peered into the darkness of the water-filled well, and thought of so many deaths that had come for nothing.

And of all the deaths to come.

CHAPTER EIGHT

It was 4:30. In four hours, more or less, Don Carlos Italla would fire his flare gun from the top of Alto Arete and the war masterminded from the clouds would commence. The only hope of stopping that signal was through the cave and up through the chimney. Even if we had had a military escort up the regular trail to the mountaintop, we still couldn't have made it on time.

We were at one end of the shortest distance between two points. And there was water in the way.

All right, I thought. Water certainly isn't impenetrable.

"Let's move the slab all the way off the well," I said, "and get some light into the damned thing. I'm going down."

"It is hopeless," Pico said. "We should spend our energies in returning to the tribal camp, in convincing Chief Botussin that we must move the camp farther into the hills, in. . ."

"Let Senor Carter go down," Purano said.

We all turned to look at him. He hadn't spoken

five words during the whole of the afternoon, not even when the guerillas had attacked. When he had been shot in the arm and thigh, he hadn't uttered a sound.

I stared at his dark eyes and wondered if he wanted me to go down to a certain death, or if he really held out hope. I couldn't read a thing in those eyes, in that deadpan face.

Five minutes later, we had the slab removed from the well and I was tying the thin, strong rope around my chest, just under my armpits.

"How far down did you climb before you came to the entrance?" I asked Pico.

"I don't remember how far," he said. "There were steps, but I don't remember it being an ordeal."

"Okay," I said, picking up a heavy rock to use as a weight. "Let me down as fast as I can sink. Play out no more than a hundred feet of rope, though. If I'm not up in sixty seconds from the time my head goes under water, pull me up, fast."

I gave my digital watch to Elicia so she could serve as timekeeper. I passed the luger and the automatic rifle over to Purano, wondering why in hell I put so much trust in him. But I wanted Pico's strong arms on that rope and I was glad to see that he took it up without being asked.

The water was cold and clear. I dropped swiftly for a few feet, then put one hand on the slippery side of the well to slow the descent. I peered around and around at the sides as I dropped with the stone in my hand. There were no breaks, no holes, no steps.

About twenty five feet down, I encountered the stone steps and could see that the steps above that point had been chiseled away. Don Carlos had planned well when he had taken to the clouds.

I had been counting in my head as I dropped through the water and searched for a break in the sides of the well. I was up to forty and still counting. I let go of the side and dropped more swiftly, wondering how far it was to the bottom and if the entrance was there.

When I hit the count of sixty, I felt the rope go taut. My eyes strained downward, hoping to catch a glimpse of the opening to the cave. I saw only the deep gloom that exists in the bottoms of all wells. But there was something different about that gloom.

As the rope began hauling me up out of the water, and as my lungs began to sear from the pain of foul air, I realized what was different below me.

There were no more steps.

The steps ended at a point about sixty feet down. As I was being hauled past the point where the steps left off, I saw a dark spot on the wall to my left, on the downhill side of the well. It was the opening.

I almost did something foolish then. I slid my stiletto into my hand and was about to cut the rope, to swim through that opening, afraid I wouldn't be able to find it again. My lungs won out over my foolishness and I was soon breaking the surface of the water and sucking in air like a landed fish.

"Did you find the opening?" Pico asked as he helped me over the rim of the well.

"I think so. It's about sixty feet down, on the left side here. Can all of you swim?"

It was a kind of stupid question to ask people who had lived their entire lives on an island. But I had to make certain. We didn't have room for anymore foulups. I described the location of the opening, just below where the steps ended.

It was decided that Pico and Purano would remain behind and stack rocks around the opening to make it look as though no one had found and entered the well. Then, they would return to the village and help the others move to the ancient campsite, just in case. Although I feared insulting the Indians and their craftsmanship, I chose the nylon rope over the hemp. It was lighter and much stronger. I taped Wilhelmina in a waterproof pouch to my back and checked to make certain Pierre and Hugo were in place. I wasn't wild about the idea of Elicia going into this impossible situation with me and the surviving four spear-chuckers, but there was no other way.

The spearchuckers themselves weren't any too happy about the arrangement. Once they comprehended the situation, they went into another whispered consultation with Purano. He frowned, then turned to me.

"They fear the curse," he said. "They refuse to go into the cave."

I had expected this, but had hoped against it. There was no way I could go into that cave and up that chimney alone. Even if I could, what possible chance would I have at the top, if I, indeed, ever reached the top? And there was no way Purano and Pico could accompany us, with their wounds. I looked at the four warriors, peering into each face in turn.

"If you don't go," I said as brutally as I could, "you'll have more than a curse to fear. Eight of your brothers died on this slope. If we remain here much longer, the red-shirted guerillas will kill the rest of you. And if they don't, I'll kill you before I go back into the water."

I meant what I had said. I had already swung a Russian rifle around toward them as I spoke. They looked to Purano for help.

"Go, or I will kill you before he has the chance."

It wasn't the sweetest of conditions, but the warriors gave grudging nods. I took the minimal amount of time to show them how to use the automatic rifles, then we were as ready as we ever would be.

"I'll go first," I said. "This time, I won't do anything to slow my descent. I'll drop as fast as the rock will take me. I'll find the opening again and swim through. If I find safe, dry land, I'll tug three times on the rope. If I don't signal within the allotted sixty seconds, pull me back up. If you pull and nothing happens, you'll know I've had it. Nobody should follow."

It would have been a safer plan for me to swim down, investigate the opening and come back to describe it in detail. But time was running out so fast that I decided on the far more dangerous aspect. It didn't matter, really. If this failed, we would all be dead within hours anyway. Or, with the elite corps in the area, within minutes.

This time, I cradled a much larger rock in my arms. As I hurtled down through the water, my ears kept popping from the sudden change in pressure. I was going so fast that I could barely see the steps flitting past.

When I reached the point where the steps ended, I tugged once on the nylon rope and immediately dropped the heavy stone. I swam upward a few feet and reached into the blackness. It was a hole. I flipped the trailing rope out of the way and swam into the hole.

The darkness was so total that I was certain I'd swum through into open space, into the mysterious Black Hole of Space. But there was nothing but blackness.

The fifty-second point passed and I felt the pain start up again in my lungs. I swam on and on. Sixty seconds. Sixty one. I felt the rope drawing tight around my armpits and knew that Pico was up there pulling, his strong arms bristling with muscles on the rope.

I was about to turn and swim with the tug of the rope when I saw a patch of light ahead and above. A lake? Impossible. I was well below the surface of the mountain. There couldn't be open water up there.

But it was something bright, something worth investigating. I pulled three times on the rope, then waited until it went slack. Our signals were working perfectly, but now I was totally on my own. If that patch of light turned out to be something other than open water, or at least a surface where I could breathe, I had no time left to swim back through the opening and up through the well.

My air was already exhausted and the pain that had begun to sear my lungs was now attacking all my joints. Everything in my body was crying out for oxygen.

My arms felt numb and tingly, almost refusing to work for me. I kept swimming, taking an upward angle toward the patch of light. The light grew in size and intensity, but it never became nearly as bright as the light at the top of the well.

And it seemed to be slipping away into the distance the farther and the harder I swam. The pain in my lungs and joints grew to a constant throbbing. I felt dizzy and disoriented, the way I had felt in special diving classes and on other assignments when I had had to swim to deep parts of the ocean. I recognized the sensation as what divers call "Raptures of the Deep." I was getting giddy and it seemed to me that it might be great fun to play with that patch of light above. I would swim almost to the surface, then dive deep again, teasing that light as though it were some benevolent animal.

Fortunately, I didn't dive. If I had, I would have instantly drowned. I broke the surface just as air came exploding from my lungs. It was an automatic spasm and the sucking in of air was just as automatic, just as involuntary. If it had happened underwater, I would have filled my lungs with water instead of air.

The light was indeed dimmer than the light outside. I was in the middle of a pool of water and there were dark rocks all around me. Above was a huge dome of a cavern. Off to one side, around an outcropping of rock, was a beam of light.

I swam to the rocks and crawled out onto what had to be the bottom of the sacrificial cave. I lay panting for several minutes and was just starting to investigate the huge cavern when something broke the water in the pond and I saw Elicia floundering near the rocky bank. She was too weak to swim any longer. I leaped back into the water and nudged her to shore.

One after another, the warriors popped up into the pond like corks from bottles. One after another, I jumped in and brought them to shore.

I waited five minutes after the last warrior was through and then began to pull on the rope, steadily but firmly.

Sure enough, Pico and Purano had tied six automatic rifles to the end of the rope. We were all armed, but we were also cut off from escape. It would have been impossible to swim back to the well without the rope to guide us.

After checking to make certain that Wilhelmina and the rifles weren't waterlogged, we began to move about the cavern. The light, we discovered, came from a wide fissure high up in the rocks. There was no way up to the fissure, so we concentrated on the center of the domed chamber. There was a raised section, like an immense stage. We climbed onto it.

As we stumbled across the stage, through the half-light of the cavern, we began to shuffle through ashes and bits of burned debris. Elicia picked up a charred object, screamed and immediately flung it down.

It was the remains of a human thigh bone.

Somewhere in this debris, I thought, were the ashes and charred bones of Pico's eleven-year-old daughter. In a way, I was glad that the giant had been wounded and wasn't along. It would have been painful for him to walk through these ashes. It was painful to me.

I couldn't take my eyes from the ashes as we walked through them. I didn't really know what I was looking for, or if I would recognize it when I saw it. And then the toe of my boot struck something that clattered.

I looked down and there it was, charred and blackened, but recognizable as a necklace made of seashells. I turned my head so that the warriors and Elicia wouldn't see the tears.

When we had reached what we determined to be the center of the immense platform, we stopped and gazed at the high dome of a ceiling. There were black smudges here and there. One of the warriors suddenly began to jabber. He was pointing to a small outcropping of rock at the center of the dome.

We moved around on the platform, looking at the outcropping from different angles. From one side we could see that a narrow opening went up through the dome. From below, it looked too small to accommodate a man, but the smoke around it clearly identified it as the start of the chimney up through the mountain.

"We have found it," Elicia said wistfully, her shoulders slumped and her face sad, "but we can do nothing. It is too high and this cave is empty of everything but rocks and bones and ashes." She shuddered.

We could have piled up rocks to give us more elevation, but that ceiling was thirty feet away. It would take days to pile up enough rocks to do us any good. By my calculations, we had just over three hours to do four hours of climbing, as it was.

The realization of failure was stronger because it also signalled our entrapment. We couldn't go forward and we couldn't go back. Our bones would be added to those in the cave, and it was no solace to us that we would not have been burned in sacrifice. Death by starvation, my boss David Hawk once said, is no damned picnic.

The four warriors also realized the hopelessness of our situation. They sat on the cold floor and began to chant in a kind of sing-song fashion that made my flesh creep. In my mind's eye, I envisioned scenes of years ago when young maidens were brought here for ceremonial torture, ceremonial sex and then ceremonial burning. I imagined that the torturers—Don Carlos leading them—had chanted in that same creepy way.

I was about ready to join them, though, when I looked up again at that outcropping of rock that had hidden the opening from us when we had first looked up. I walked around in a circle, kicking burned bones aside, studying that piece of jutting rock.

It stuck out from the ceiling at right angles, spearing across a corner of the hole. And I could see that the hole was bigger than we had first thought. There was ample room for a man to get past that outcropping, that spear of rock, and into the chimney.

But how was a person to get up to the jutting piece of rock?

The answer was still tied around my chest. I looked down at the rope trailing away into the darkness. It was thin, but it was strong. And it was supple.

"What are you doing?" Elicia asked as I began coiling up the loose end of the rope.

"I'm going to play cowboy," I said, grinning at her. "Just watch."

The four warriors stopped their chanting to watch my strange activities. I tied a loop in the end of the rope and coiled about forty feet of it around my shoulder. I took a few practice throws, but the loop never rose more than twenty feet in the air. The warriors and Elicia were looking at me as though I'd lost my senses.

"All right," I said, grinning at them as I coiled the rope for another throw. "That's enough practice. Now I go for the real thing."

"For what real thing?" Elicia asked.

"Just watch."

I went for the outcropping of rock. The lariat arched up through the air and missed the rock by inches. The warriors, not understanding what I was trying to do and convinced that I'd gone daft, began their chant again. Elicia suspected the truth and began to bite her lower lip and give body English to the trajectory of the lariat.

On the fifth try, the loop snaked over the end of the rock spear and I tugged gently on the rope. The loop tightened, but it was far out near the end of the rock, at its weakest point. The chances of the rock supporting my weight were sparse, but I had no other choice.

I put more weight on the rope and the loop tightened more. Pebbles came loose somewhere up there and rained down on us. The warriors chanted louder and began to howl. Elicia bit her lip so hard that I expected to see blood spurt out.

The suspense was also killing me. I took a chance then. I lifted myself by the rope, felt a ping in my side from my wound, and began to swing back and forth across the platform of old bones. The warriors let out a cheer. They finally understood the principle of the lariat. They also were hoping that I was more powerful than the curse put on the cave. I'd try not to disappoint them.

But we were far from out of it. I climbed a few feet on the rope, my eyes on that slender point of rock that jutted out beside the chimney hole. I flopped about, testing the strength of the rock, then began a swift, hand-over-hand climb.

When I was ten feet off the ground, I heard a fluttering sound and thought perhaps the whole ceiling was starting to crack open above me. I saw nothing. The rock was holding and the ceiling had no new cracks in it. I climbed faster.

I reached the twenty foot level when the fluttering came again, louder, more menacing, closer.

"Look out, Nick," Elicia screamed.

Her voice echoed through the chamber and seemed to come at me from a hundred different directions. I looked up and saw why she had shouted.

Something huge and black and pulsating had dropped from the chimney and was zooming straight down toward me. I thought at first that it was a great glob of soot, then I thought of a soot-blackened boulder.

But why was it pulsating?

The black glob was about to hit me when it seemed to break apart with a great fluttering sound. I nearly let go of the rope. My heart was pounding several hundred miles an hour. I let out a yip of my own and heard the cries and shouts of Elicia and the warriors below.

But I held tight to the rope and tried to duck my head away from the falling glob. The fluttering sound rose and seemed like thunder in my ears. Small black objects were zooming around my head and off to distant parts of the cave. Soft wings beat at me.

And then I knew.

Bats.

The cave had been strangely absent of life when we had entered it, but that opening that provided light should have told me that wildlife of some sort must be using this cave. That wildlife was bats and they had all been in their favorite nest in the opening of the chimney.

That black glob that had looked like a soot-covered boulder was a cluster of several hundred bats.

Elicia was screaming below me, but I knew she was in no danger. She was merely reacting to the bats that were now streaking back and forth in the cave, dive-bombing every alien object spotted by their special radar. While the bats occupied themselves with harrassing Elicia and the warriors, I continued my climb to the top of the rope.

My side was on fire and every muscle in my body—especially my hands—threatened to go soft on me as I took one hand from the rope and clasped it around the rock spear. The spear, I could see in the dim light, actually was the leading edge of a small ledge just outside the hole leading up.

There were hundreds of baby bats in a nest on that ledge.

A high-pitched squeal came from the nest when my hand bumped against it. This set off the other bats in the cave. They were still streaking back and forth, dive-bombing Elicia and the four warriors. Now they began a screeching and squealing that was almost deafening, and was certainly hair-raising.

Distasteful as it was, I raised myself with both hands on the rock ledge and reached in to scoop out the nest. Bony wings flapped against my arm and face as the debris came falling down past me. Straw, twigs, dried grass and large cakes of bat shit made up most of the debris.

The screeching in the cave reached a fever pitch when the baby bats went plummeting down to the platform. The adult bats began swooping down and catching the little ones in wiry claws, then flying around and around in a circle, looking for a safe place to nest them. But I had fought hard for this place at the peak of the cave's dome and I wasn't about to be unseated by mama bats.

It took several minutes, however, to work my way up through the hole and onto the ledge. The hole was bigger than it had looked from below.

There was plenty of room for me to stand on the ledge, haul the others up one by one with the rope and let them get past me into the chimney.

I looked up to see if other ledges existed above me, but the walls were smooth and black. I stood on the ledge and ran my hands over the smooth walls of the almost round hole. Soot fell away, covering my body and falling down into the cave.

The only way to climb, I deduced, would be to put my feet on one side of the wall and my back against the other. By scooting along, like a mountain climber in a narrow ravine or cleft, I'd be able to make progress. It would be slow progress, but I knew the chimney must narrow as it rose. It must also twist and turn, giving us purchase with our feet and hands.

Then again, I thought, this isn't a man-made hole up through the mountain. Smoke and air don't need large or perfect openings. The chimney might have places where it narrowed too much to permit the passage of anything the size of a man.

There was, of course, only one way to find answers to all my speculations. And that was to climb up.

I was tempted to go on alone, knowing that time was precious and that I could make much better time on my own. But I would need the warriors and Elicia at the top. I would need firepower. That is, if this chimney had an opening at the top big enough for us to get through.

I loosened the loop of rope on the jutting rock and made a more secure link over a greater section of rock. When the rope was ready, I looked down and saw that Elicia and the four warriors were still fending off bats.

"Climb up first, Elicia," I shouted. "The rope is secure."

"Nick, I can't do it," she shouted back. "The bats. They're attacking our eyes."

I looked harder and sure enough the bats were not missing them in their diving attacks. Most were still swooping past Elicia and the others, but some —perhaps the mothers of the disenfranchised babies—were making direct hits, going for the eyes.

I remembered reading somewhere that bats were frightened of loud noises. The sound of our voices had alarmed them and had got them stirred up. What would a louder sound do to them?

I didn't know, but anything was worth a try. I got Wilhelmina out of its pouch and aimed at a point to the side of the platform. It wouldn't do to have a ricochet or a hunk of splintered rock hit Elicia or the others.

BOOM!

The whole damned cave seemed to explode in a rolling crescendo of thunder. The sound of the shot echoed from wall to wall and back again, nearly blasting out my eardrums. I could imagine what the sound must have been like below.

The bats went wild then. The deafening sound of the luger shot must have fritzed up their radar. They screeched and slammed into the walls of the cave. The mothers gave up their attack on Elicia and the warriors and went sailing off into walls. Some of them even flopped into the icy pond and a few others sailed out through the narrow opening into the afternoon light.

"Hurry and climb," I called down. "Once they get their senses back, they'll renew their attack. Come on, Elicia."

Elicia climbed as though she'd been squirreling up ropes all her life. She reached the outcropping of rock and I put out a hand to help her. She missed my hand on the first try and did a crazy spiral on the rope. Her hand slashed at the air and she was about to lose her grip with her other hand. I leaned down, caught her swirling arm and literally dragged her into the hole and onto the narrow ledge.

"Climb farther up to make room for the others," I said. "Put your feet against one side and your back against the other. Just scoot your body along until you're ten to fifteen feet up the tunnel."

She was short and her body barely gained purchase on the opposing walls. When she went past me, I put my hands on her buttocks to give her a boost. Her skirt was hanging free and my hands were against bare flesh. For a fleeting moment, I remembered that delicious hour in the council hut, then put it all out of my mind. Wrong time, wrong place. And she was Purano's woman now.

Most of the rest went smoothly and without mishap. But not all. When three of the warriors were shuttling along up after Elicia and the fourth was on the rope, climbing up, the bats returned.

"Hurry, before their radar picks you out," I said in a hoarse whisper. "Climb, man, climb."

The Indian came streaking up the rope, hand over hand, his legs dangling free. The bats sensed him and, after making several swoops just beneath him, they zeroed in on his body and, finally, his face.

He was almost at the top when a huge bat came swooping in a wide arc around the full circumference of the cave below. It took a radar bead on the warrior's eyes and scored a direct hit just as my hand was touching the Indian's outstretched hand.

We never made the proper link.

The warrior let out a scream, and let go of the rope. The bats skittered to dark areas of the cave and I lunged forward to catch the man's flailing arms. I missed and he went plummeting thirty feet through the dimly-lighted air.

I heard him hit, heard the sickening thwack of skull being cracked open. I knew he was dead the moment he landed. But I waited there at the opening to make sure. The Indian had landed on his head, and his rifle had gone clattering across the platform, sending up a cloud of ashes. Human ashes. I stared at his body, at the grotesque way he was strewn on the platform. There was no movement and the bats were already attacking his face.

Even as a sick feeling was rumbling through my stomach and chest, I looked up to see that the others had also witnessed the disaster. The three warriors and Elicia were silent, watching the bats work over the battered corpse below. I didn't try to imagine what they were thinking or feeling: there was no time for the obvious.

But I did respect their feelings and thoughts. I waited until they had obviously prayed for the soul of the dead warrior and then I began to climb slowly past them.

"I'll take the lead," I said as I edged past the three warriors in the channel. "We'll have to hurry now."

"How much time do we have?" Elicia asked as I eased past her.

I took my digital watch from its waterproof pouch and saw that it was still running. The numbers flipped over to 5:32.

"We have just about three hours," I said. "We'll have to really punish ourselves and keep at it."

"Do you think the bats will return?"

"I doubt it," I said, although I didn't doubt it for a minute. "The way should be clear and easy now."

It wasn't.

As I moved up into a narrow channel and saw that it split into two equal-sized holes, I heard movement above. A soft buzzing sound came from the hole to my left. I flipped on my flashlight and examined the hole openings. Soot covered the walls of both holes, so both apparently were open. I played the light into the left hole, trying to see what was making the buzzing sound, but could see only a twisting, turning, soot-covered channel ahead. The hole on the right presented an identical sight, but it had no buzzing sound in it.

I took the hole to the right. I hadn't gone five feet into it, though, when I realized that it was narrowing radically. I no longer could maintain purchase with my feet against one side and my back against the other. I reached out and found small ledges in the darkness above. I let my feet hang free and began to climb the ledges with my fingertips. It was rough going, but I knew it would be easier once my feet were inside the hole and I could use my feet on the ledges.

I never got that far. The hole narrowed until my shoulders were touching the sides. Soon, I couldn't get my shoulders through. I started crawling back down.

Meanwhile, below me, one of the warriors had seen me go into the right-side hole and had decided to take the left. He had edged past Elicia and was climbing up into the hole where I had heard the soft buzzing.

"Hold it," I said, tapping his foot just as he was lifting it to a small ledge inside the hole. "We'd better find out what's buzzing first."

"No problem, Senor," he said, his voice muffled in the narrow hole. "The buzzing is only flies making a nest. I clean them out good."

Elicia, the other two warriors and I propped our bodies in the wider channel below and waited for the intrepid warrior to clean out the nest of flies. It was good to rest, though I was conscious of the digital watch flipping over numbers as precious time went by.

From above came a louder buzzing, as though the warrior was stirring up the flies. I heard a low curse from the warrior, then a furious buzzing, then a scream from the hole.

"Aaaaiiiiiieeeeee!"

The man's feet began to thrash in the hole and the warrior slipped down until he was almost kicking me in the face. He screamed again and I reached out to support his legs. He kicked me twice alongside the head and I was ready to scream myself when the buzzing grew louder and I felt soft furry things falling down across my head, face and chest. They dropped into the gloom below.

"Scorpions!" the warrior shouted between screams. "A nest of scorpions! They're stinging me!"

He screamed again as another scorpion obviously stung him up in that hole. I pulled on the man's legs and brought him down out of the hole. Three large scorpions were skittering across his upper body and he was almost white with shock. I batted away the scorpions and, with Elicia's help, we nestled him against the wall between us. He was no longer screaming, but a low moaning sound was rattling constantly from his lips. His face and arms were swollen from scorpion stings.

The poison from a single scorpion normally isn't

enough to kill a man, or even to incapacitate him immediately, but this man had received several stings. I had no idea how many and there wasn't time to strip him there in the channel. The point was, he was of no use to us now: he was a liability. We would have to carry him, in spite of the fact that it was becoming even more difficult to continue without having anything or anyone to carry.

It wasn't easy to generate compassion for the man who was obviously dying in my arms. I considered his great pain and the shock of the poison, but I kept thinking of him as a liability, an impossible burden.

"He is dead," Elicia said, looking up from the warrior's face. Her small hand was across his forehead. He was indeed motionless, his lips no longer letting out that unintelligible moaning. "What can we do now, Nick? We cannot go on and we cannot go back?"

I was about at the end of my endurance. I had no desire to climb into that nest of scorpions that still remained in the hole on our left, and the other hole obviously was too small to get through. I was sore and raw from scraping against the rough walls of the hole. I was exhausted from the day's strenuous activities—I still hadn't recovered from that frightening swim before we had begun the climb up this impossible chimney. And the shocks to my emotions, from the bats, from the brutal death of the first warrior and from the tightening suspense of knowing that Don Carlos Italla might start his war while we were still burrowing up through the mountain like moles were taking a rigorous toll. And the newly-dead warrior was getting heavier by the minute.

I wanted to let go, to just make my body and my

mind go slack. I wanted to drop through space, back down the incredible chimney and join the broken warrior on the sacrificial platform far below.

"What can we do?" Elicia asked again.

I didn't have an answer for her. In addition to physical exhaustion and emotional shock, I felt tremendously frustrated, as though I'd been involved in a series of impossible tests and wasn't passing any of them. And the dead Indian being supported by Elicia and I was gradually slipping down the smooth wall of the chimney.

Thoughts of just plain giving up were running rampant in my mind. Such thoughts must be amazingly close to those experienced by a person just before he commits suicide. At that moment, giving up meant committing suicide. On the other hand, my mind told me—actually screamed at me—going on was just as suicidal.

A great deal of my past life flashed through my mind in staccato bursts, like quick images of filmed replays. I saw myself in previously "hopeless" situations, saw how I had come out of them alive and triumphant. In my many years as N3, as Killmaster for AXE, such hopeless situations were legion, but I had experienced innumerable miracles to bring me out of them.

There was no miracle at hand this time. No light in the water ahead. No retreat. No weapon that could destroy the nest of scorpions above us without destroying us in the process.

"Nick?" Elicia said, her voice rising in panic as she recognized the look of total defeat on my face. "We must do something. We must do it soon. I feel myself giving out. I can't hold on much longer."

"Neither can I, Elicia," I said, looking at her sadly, helplessly. "Neither can I."

CHAPTER NINE

Years ago, when I was sitting in the anteroom of AXE's offices on DuPont Circle in Washington, waiting to report on the completion of an assignment, a secretary had inadvertently left open the intercom to David Hawks's office. I heard my old boss tell someone in there:

"If ever AXE comes up with a truly impossible assignment, one that could not possibly be handled by a mortal with a mortal's powers and intelligence, one that could not be handled by man's most sophisticated weaponry or technology, one that could be resolved only by divine intervention or by the gods themselves, I would give that assignment to Nick Carter and fully expect him to resolve it."

I remember the response from Hawk's unknown visitor: "Nobody is that good."

"True," Hawk had said. "Nobody is that good, not even Nick Carter. But he thinks he's that good and, after all, isn't that all that's necessary in any assignment, impossible or otherwise?"

Well, perched there in that filthy hole of a chimney with my body wracked with pain, my back and knees raw, a dead warrior in my arms, a nest of impenetrable scorpions just above me, a water-filled cave entrance far below me and a virtual army of fanatics on top of the mountain, I suddenly realized that that intercom hadn't been left open accidentally. It had been done on purpose. I had been conned into thinking that, even if nobody was good enough for a particular assignment, I was fully expected to complete it successfully.

I realized something else, I really *wasn't* good enough, not for this one. It had been a stacked deck against me all along. I had come this far through sheer luck and brashness and downright foolhardiness. And where had I come? To my own death trap, that's where.

"Nick?" Elicia cried, more panic in her voice. "Nick, I'm slipping. I can't hold on any longer."

All right, I thought. I don't know what to do, but I'm expected to do something. David Hawk had expected it all along and had gotten the results he desired. Elicia expected it. The two warriors waiting just below expected it. Even if my next move were a wrong move, I had to make it.

"We'll have to drop him," I said to Elicia. "It seems cruel, but the man is dead and won't feel a thing. Let him go." I looked down at the waiting warriors. "Take the body and let it fall back down the chimney."

They were aghast at the thought, and their faces showed it, but they took their comrade as Elicia and I eased him down. They held him for a few minutes, then reluctantly let him go. We gritted our teeth and held our positions in that narrow chimney and listened to the smacking, crunching, grinding sounds as the man and his rifle dropped all the way down and slammed into the sacrificial platform two hundred feet below.

And what next? When the warrior had first run into the scorpion nest, I had considered using one of my gas bombs to rout them. But the plan had some unpleasant ramifications.

For one thing, in that closed area the gas would spread out in a cloud and engulf us all. I knew from experience that no man could hold his breath long enough for the gas to disperse. Secondly, the gas might linger in the tunnel above us, especially if there were level areas up there. And a third thing: gas would escape at the top of the chimney, and might be detected by forces up there, forces who would know immediately that someone was coming up the chimney.

A plan began to hatch in my head as I rested there and felt a soft breeze waft upwards past my body. It wasn't a perfect plan, but no plan is.

"Move back down the chimney," I said to Elicia and the two remaining warriors. "Go down about a hundred feet and wait for me."

"But there's no time," Elicia protested.

"I know. We're not interested in stopping Don Carlos any longer. We're interested in survival. Forget the time."

Even as they moved back down the chimney, though, I knew that I hadn't meant that about not being interested in stopping Don Carlos. That was the main objective and my years of training wouldn't let my mind forget it, not even for the moment, for self-survival.

When Elicia and the two warriors were out of

sight, I took a smooth, sleek little Pierre from a pouch on my thigh and tied the end of the nylon rope to the pin. I worked the bomb into a niche in the rocks, tested to make sure it wouldn't come away easily, then moved back down the chimney. When I had gone fifty feet, I found a small ledge and began to load the contents of my pocket onto it. I crumpled up all the money in my billfold into a heap. I took out my passport and my identification card and a bunch of other cards I carry around for a number of reasons: my blood donor card to remind me that I am also human; my library card to remind that civilization really does have its finer side; my credit cards to remind me that civilization has another side; my health insurance card to remind me that I'm not (as Hawk's friend suggested) invincible; some receipts and notes to remind me that life has a quiet aspect to it at times. I put the wallet itself on the pile.

I remembered that my notebook had been put in the pouch with Wilhelmina. I recovered it and tore out the page containing the map I'd drawn of Alto Arete's fortifications. I then tore out all the other pages, crumpled them up and put them on the pile. I tucked the folded map back into the pouch.

Next, I took out Hugo and began to slice long splinters off the butt of the Russian automatic rifle. It was soft wood and I thanked the Russians for cheapening up in such a way. The wood had a fragrance to it, like cedar. It would burn well. I cut several short lengths of nylon rope and added them to the pile, then took apart a half dozen bullets and shook gunpowder over the whole thing. I found two extra books of matches and, only as a last resort when I was certain they were needed to make the fire more effective, I added my last box of goldmonogramed Turkish cigarettes.

When I had eased below the ledge to keep the gunpowder from flashing in my face, I lit a match and flipped it up onto the pile. The flash was instant and blinding. I moved back down the chimney and watched as the flames built and set up eerie shadows in the space above me.

It took less than a minute before I felt an increase in the wind moving up past me. The fire was creating a fine draft, as I expected it to in this narrow chimney. I watched, waiting for the flames to reach a peak, but carefully watching to see that it didn't burn the length of nylon rope that I had tied to Pierre and snaked down past the ledge holding the fire.

When I was certain that the upward draft was at optimum force, I yanked on the nylon. I heard the familiar pop as Pierre burst open in the closed space well above the fire. I sucked in my breath and held it, still watching the fire on the ledge a dozen feet above. There was hardly a flicker in the flames from the explosion of the gas bomb and I knew I was safe.

The draft created by the fire, had swept all the gas upward. The draft would also clear the gas out of level tunnels and other pockets where it might otherwise collect.

Best of all, the gas would infiltrate that nest of scorpions and, unless they were capable of holding their breaths for the next few minutes, wipe the nest clean of life.

But I was still worried about what might happen on top of the mountain when they saw the blue cloud of gas and the white smoke. As I said, the plan wasn't perfect.

I gave the fire another five minutes, then called

down to Elicia and the warriors. Even as Elicia responded, I felt something soft and furry land on my shoulder. I started to brush it off, then realized what it was. I shone my flashlight on it and saw that it was a scorpion.

It was deader than hell.

"What did you do?" Elicia asked as she drew up behind me. I was putting out the fire so we could go past the ledge without being burned.

"Made a few sacrifices of my own" I said, thinking of the lost money and library card. They represented a small loss compared to Pico's daughter and all those other victims of Don Carlos Italla's idiocy, but a sacrifice, nonetheless.

As we moved upward, brushing aside dead scorpions from the now defunct nest, I explained to Elicia what I had done and she showered me with so many compliments that I began to wonder what David Hawk would say when he heard my report on the clearing of the scorpions. I knew what he would say, to the word:

"Standard operating procedure, N3. Why did it take you so long to think of it?"

It is sometimes depressing working for a man like David Hawk. But only sometimes.

Our only obstacles now were time and a flagging of strength. As we continued to climb the chimney, knocking away more nests of dead scorpions and spiders and other denizens of the dark chimney that runs straight up through the mountain to Alto Arete, the air seemed thinner and less satisfying to breathe. But it was clean air now, thanks to the draft from the fire; and the tunnel was clear of life-threatening creatures, thanks to Pierre's lethal draft.

We no longer could inch our way up by using

our backs and knees against opposing walls. The
hole had narrowed so much that my shoulders
barely cleared its sides. We used tiny notches and
ledges and, in some stretches, found the walls so
smooth that we actually wriggled like snakes to
gain upward purchase.

We did run across several level areas where we
could rest, but I kept looking at my digital watch,
seeing the minutes flick away. The numbers seemed
to be constantly changing. 7:45. 7:59. 8:05.

I lost all sense of place and had no idea how far
we had come from the cave. It could have been five
hundred feet, or five thousand. I knew only that
sundown was rushing across the island and that
Don Carlos would soon step onto a balcony of his
palace up there on Alto Arete and fire his flare,
signalling the beginning of a bloody revolution that
would rock the island from end to end, side to side.
Once that started, I would not have an ally in the
whole country. All the Ninca Indians would be
dead, as would the guerillas who opposed Don
Carlos.

Without allies, I knew, there was no way for me
to get off the island country of Nicarxa. There
would be no report to David Hawk or the President because there would be no one to report.

"What time is it?" Elicia asked as we rested in a
narrow tunnel that angled upwards at about forty
five degrees.

"Almost eight o'clock," I lied. I had been lying
about the time for the past two hours. Even though
I'd told her earlier that we were no longer concerned with Don Carlos Italla's plans but with our
own survival, I knew she didn't accept that anymore than I did. She still hoped to stop the maniac
and save her country from a bloodbath. I had tried

once to shatter that hope, when my own hope was
at rock bottom—I wouldn't do it again. But I
looked at my watch and saw that the numbers were
clearly at 8:12.

"Do you think we're near the top?" Elicia asked.

"I'm pretty sure we are," I said.

This time, I wasn't lying. For the past several
yards, the chimney had been getting narrower and
narrower. I could barely squeeze my shoulders past
small outcroppings. And I noticed that a number
of smaller holes ran off into different directions. I
had the sickening feeling that the chimney would
degenerate into a series of tiny openings through
which only smoke (and poison gas) could pass.

The feeling was justified. Just as my digital
watch clicked into place at 8:15, I shone my
flashlight ahead and saw that the main chimney ten
feet ahead was no wider than a man's boot. Smaller
chimneys led off from the channel like dark fingers,
each about the size of a fist.

I stopped and probed the area above, but could
find no way for us to get through. It was possible
that this series of smaller holes represented only a
small section of the overall chimney, that they fun-
neled into a main chimney up above. The question
was, how did we get past this natural obstruction
to the main chimney?

What was needed now, I knew, was that divine
intervention David Hawk had spoken of. I had no
weapons to deal with the situation. As a matter of
fact, no sophisticated weaponry or technology
could solve this problem in time for us to stop Don
Carlos.

I reached the point where my shoulders would
no longer let themselves be squeezed any closer together. Ahead, the main chimney narrowed like

dark railroad tracks in the distance. This time, though, the narrowing was no optical illusion. It was real.

We could go no farther.

"Why do you stop, Nick?" Elicia said. "We still have time to stop Don Carlos, but we must not stop. Not now."

Truth time.

There was no way I could lie my way out of this predicament. I would have to tell her and the two warriors that we were stopped, that we could not proceed. Pierre couldn't help. Hugo couldn't help. Wilhelmina could blast away forever and make no dent at all in the obstacle ahead.

Nick Carter had failed. Oh, sure, there might be people in the future who might say I had given it my best shot. That is, if any of us got out alive to tell the story. Even if they said I gave it my best shot, they'd still have to sigh and shake their heads and finish the statement: "Even though he gave it his best shot, he still failed."

"Nick, are you all right? Why have we stopped?"

I couldn't answer, couldn't tell her. I wanted to. I wanted to tell her that I expected failure all along, that I had been proceeding like a damned programmed automation, a brainless creature destined to smash itself on the rocks of total adversity, of hopelessness.

My fingers sought a higher ledge. My mind entertained the hope of squeezing my shoulders just a bit tighter, of going on; hope that the chimney would widen in just a few more feet and we would be able to continue to the top.

The hope, however, was faint and dim. What was really going through my mind was just how we four would spend our remaining hours alive.

Would we talk among ourselves as hunger turned to starvation, as life began to seep away leaving our bones as evidence to some future archeologist that we had been here? Would that archeologist puzzle about our predicament, have any hint at all as to why we had wedged ourselves into this incredible mountain?

Hope was still alive and my fingers kept searching for one more ledge.

My mind, however, was still active in other areas. It was possible, I thought, that we could go back down to the cave and subsist on bats until desperation drove us to that dark pond and that impossible swim back to the well. We could eat scorpions. There were a lot of dead ones down there. We could eat the two warriors who had died in this hopeless endeavor. We. . .

"We're in deep trouble, aren't we?" Elicia said, the panic coming again to her voice. "We can't go any farther, can we?"

My fingers found a narrow depression in the rock. I didn't want to have to answer Elicia. I probed the depression and tried to get my fingertips into it. It wasn't a ledge and it wasn't deep enough to provide purchase. I kept trying.

"Answer me, Nick." We're trapped and it's almost time for Don Carlos to send his signal and I can't even find a ledge to pull me higher into this damned hole and we're going to die here while all your countrymen are dying outside. I opened my mouth to tell them all the truth, but I couldn't find my voice.

I was incapable, in that moment of frustration and failure, to admit that I was frustrated, that I had failed. My fingers worked frantically in the narrow depression. I slid my hands across the depression and found that it was a straight line, as though it had been chiseled there by man and not by nature.

"You don't have to answer," Elicia said, a slight choking in her throat. "Your silence tells me everything."

"I'm just thinking, Elicia," I said, lying again, although it wasn't a total lie. I *was* thinking. I was thinking about how bats and scorpions and human flesh would taste to a man about to perish of starvation.

"I want to tell you," Elicia said, a braveness in her voice now, "that I cherish those moments in the Council House. I am in love with Purano and would have married him and bore his children, but I would not have forgotten my love for you, for what we had together."

"Elicia, don't talk like that. You're giving up."

"Haven't you given up?"

I pushed against the rock wall just below the depression, a new hope rising. Nothing happened.

"No, I haven't given up. There's no reason to give up."

"Then, why won't you answer my questions? Why don't we continue on?"

I pushed hard against the rock wall, then slid my hands down the wall close to my chest. I found another faint line there, another slight depression. I worked my fingers across it, gouging out crumpled rock. It was another straight line and the crumpling rock felt like mortar in my hands.

Mortar? Here, near the top of a natural chimney? I worked the stone dust in my fingers and tasted it. As comparison, I licked the natural rock wall in front of me. The tastes were different.

Elicia was crying softly now, but my mind was

too busy with the new puzzle to give time to comfort her. I had nothing yet with which to comfort her—perhaps I never would.

I probed the wall and traced the lines that ran parallel about eighteen inches apart. I found corners, then began to trace lines that ran vertically. It was a square. A square of lines filled with what might be mortar. A sealed opening or door? Impossible? Yes, impossible. My mind in its desperation was playing morbid tricks on me.

In a tiny part of my mind, I had retained hope that there would be a kind of door or other man-made opening at or near the top of this natural chimney. Of course, the same part of my mind that hoped for the opening also held out the distinct possibility that that opening would be heavily guarded.

What lay behind this square of stone sealed with crumpling mortar? Or, my mind swerved from that grim possibility, what made me think I'd be able to break the seal and get this stone unseated? How thick was the stone and did they have something even heavier and thicker directly behind it?

Relying on that thin hope, I took Hugo from his sheath and began tracing the thin point of the stiletto around the squared lines. I had given up using the sharp weapon to get myself and the others out of this predicament. I made a silent apology to the vicious little knife.

"Nick, what are you doing?" Elicia asked, between sobs. "Are you trying to cut your way through solid stone?"

"That, my sweet," I said, chuckling as renewed hope rose to a crescendo in my soul, "is a fairly adequate description of precisely what I'm doing."

I heard one of the warriors mutter something

that sounded like "loco," but I went on slashing at the cracks. Mortar by the handful fell past me and showered Elicia and the two warriors. I knew I would be able to loosen the mortar and possibly push the square stone out of its socket in the wall, but what then?

Even if there were no guards behind this wall and even if Don Carlos hadn't yet signalled for the revolution to begin, what chance had one exhausted gringo, a sobbing girl and two disconsolate and disenchanted Indians against the formidible bastion described by Luis Pequeno, the Cuban Marine whose story had set me on this fantastic voyage up through the center of the mountain?

No matter, I thought. One thing at a time. If I were concerned about how to stop Don Carlos once I reached his lair in the clouds, I should have resolved the matter long ago, not now. Now was the time for action, any action, to get out of this dark trap and to do all that was humanly possible to complete the mission.

When Hugo's thin blade could find no more loose stone and mortar to unseat, I put him back in his sheath and leaned as far away from the square as possible. I put the palms of both hands against the stone and gave a push. It didn't budge. I pushed harder, grunting like an animal in heat, but the stone was unmovable. I rested, took time to look at my watch—it stood at 8:20 now—and explained to Elicia what I was trying to do, then gave the one final shot of my strength. It still didn't move. The watch numbers flicked to 8:24. Sweat, spurred by physical exertion and growing panic, mixed with the soot, spider webs and mortar on my face and hands.

I had no energy to give the stone much of a push

now. I had used it up. Perhaps a rest of five minutes or so would restore it, but each passing minute meant a greater risk of failure, if we hadn't already failed.

It was then that I heard the faint clanking sound from behind the stone. I felt the stone move against my chest. I put my palms against it, took a deep breath and willed my strength to return without a proper rest.

I pushed as hard as I could. The stone moved a fraction of an inch and I felt that it wasn't me that had moved it. Someone was tugging from the other side. I understood the clanking sound then. Don Carlos had undoubtedly fitted the stone with a metal handle of some sort, in case he needed to remove it and use the chimney as an escape route.

Someone was in there tugging on that metal handle. That someone was obviously not a friend, but an enemy who had heard me scraping away with Hugo and was curious to see what was happening in the chimney.

Again, I thought, it's no matter. Friend or foe, I'm coming through.

I heard the clank again, felt the stone start to move. I timed my final push with that, gave it all I had, and the stone popped out of that square like the cork from a bottle of exquisite champagne.

Even as the stone was falling away and I was peering into a dimly-lit chamber beyond, I had Wilhelmina in my hand. The stone plummeted to the floor of the chamber and I saw a short man in monk's garb scrambling out of its way. He still had his hand on the metal handle he'd been tugging on.

I leaped through the opening and stared at the startled monk. I took a look around and saw that we were in an enormous wine cellar. The monk had let go of the handle and was lying on his backside, staring up with wide eyes at the big pistol in my hand.

"El diablo," he gasped.

"No," I said, "not the devil, but somebody just as determined. And if you don't cooperate right now, my friend, this someone is determined to blow your head off. Tell me, has Don Carlos sent the signal yet?"

I could hear Elicia and the two warriors coming through the hole behind me, and could tell by the monk's face that they were entering the room. His eyes grew wider, as though he had seen more devils. We must have looked terrifying with our faces, hands and clothing smudged with soot and other assorted debris from the chimney.

"What signal, senor?" the monk asked.

I put the cold muzzle of the luger to his forehead and slid back the ejection chamber. I tightened my finger on the trigger.

"This devil isn't kidding around, pal," I said. "You know what signal. I'll give you one more chance, then I pull the trigger."

He sweated and squirmed a little, then he seemed to recognize one of the warriors with me. He squinted at the warrior and a smile played at his lips.

"Uturo?" he said.

The warrior nodded. "I am Uturo. Who are you?"

"Sagacio," the monk said. "I am your father's brother. I am your uncle."

"No," the warrior said. "Sagacio was killed when I was ten years old."

"So they told you," the monk said. He was smiling openly now. He started to get up, looked cross-eyed at the business end of Wilhelmina and changed his mind. "I got drunk one night on wine," he went on, "and fell in with some of our tribe that had already joined Don Carlos and his rabble. When I sobered up, I was their captive. I was brought here a dozen years ago and have been here ever since."

The warrior studied the chunky monk for a time, then leaned down and took the man's hand. He slid up the coarse robe and peered at a wide scar just below the biceps. He smiled then and looked at me.

"It is Sagacio. It is my uncle. He got that wound on a boar hunt. I remember it."

Old Sagacio began to ramble on then, about other mutual memories, but I had to put a stop to it. I had already put the luger in my belt and the old monk had raised from his undignified position, no longer afraid of the devils from the chimney.

"Has Don Carlos sent the signal?" I asked again.

"No," the monk said, shaking his head. "There is a storm and the entire mountain is covered with clouds. Don Carlos is furious with the weather, even though it is passing to the southwest. The clouds will be gone in a few minutes and he will send the signal then."

"And what are you doing down here?" I asked, looking around the wine cellar again. "Planning to get drunk again?"

"No, I was sent to fetch more wine for Don Carlos. As I said, he is furious with the storm and has been drinking steadily ever since it started."

A thought struck me.

"If you came for wine for your master, knowing that he's furious and will probably be even more pissed off if you don't hurry, why did you take time to pull on that stone?"

Segacio looked sheepish, then the look turned to one of shrewdness.

"I have sought escape ever since I was brought here," he said. "Many of Don Carlos Italla's earlier followers and all of his captives despise the man now. He is not a man of god, but a man of satan. We all look for ways of escape."

"And they all know about the sacrificial cave and the legendary chimney?"

"Yes. When we are sent for wine, we each keep trying to pull out that stone. Don Carlos says that the area behind it is inhabited by devils who will cut out our tongues and lead us to hell. Still, we chance it. When I heard you digging, I felt that my chance had come. I pulled and pulled, and it finally came out."

I had another thought. It was the constant pulling by the monks that had loosened the mortar at the back end of the stone. If not for them, I would never have found those depressions, those squared lines. Such things are not accidents, I realize. Fate, perhaps, but not accidents. Perhaps fate had other good things in store.

"How many of Don Carlos's people feel the same as you? How many can we count on as allies?"

"Allies in what?" Sagacio asked, his face screwing up with puzzlement.

"We've come to stop him," I said, "to stop the war, to end his reign from this cloudy mountaintop."

Sagacio looked at us, mentally counting our forces against those of his master.

"We started out with a larger force," I told him, "but things happened along the way. Now, will you help us? Are there others who will help?"

"What is it you wish from us? We will help."

I took out the map I had drawn with Luis Pequeno's assistance, and spread it on the ground. Sagacio took a torch from a distant wallhanger and brought it close.

"Is this an accurate map of what's on top of the mountain?" I asked.

"As far as it goes," he said. "Below ground here are the wine cellars which are extensive. Off that way, down that tunnel, is the central arsenal." He pointed to a corridor cut into the stone. "Don Carlos has Russian munitions there, much TNT and dynamite. Up that way—" he pointed to a stone staircase—" is the main guard station where a dozen armed men are on duty at all times."

"Are they from your tribe?"

"No, they are guerillas from the regular population. Some of them hate Don Carlos, but I'm not certain of which would be a friend or which would be an ally."

"All right," I said. "Here's what you do. Take the wine to Don Carlos, then return to the guard station. If you recognize any guard that might be a friend, take him aside and tell him to distract the other guards in some way. Get them away from the station. We'll go past the station, make our way to the palace and see if we can take Don Carlos hostage. If we succeed, his friends will be helpless and you can start organizing his enemies to keep his friends from rushing us. Can you do that?"

"If I have a weapon."

I gave him the Russian rifle I'd been whittling on to make my fire down there on that ledge, when I'd set off Pierre to kill the scorpions. He grinned shrewdly and slipped the rifle up under his smock. I looked at my digital watch. It stood at 8:37.

"We'll come up in ten minutes," I said. "Make sure you've done your work then."

"I will make sure."

When he was gone, I went over the plan with the two warriors—Uturo and the man whose name I still couldn't remember. It was a simple plan. We'd move past the guard station, across the main plaza to the palace, circle to a side door, kill the guard with Hugo, slip into the palace and make our way to Don Carlos's quarters.

"And what will I do?" Elicia asked.

"Stay down here," I said. "The three of us can do it, with help from Uturo's uncle."

A door slammed behind us and we all four nearly jumped out of our clothes. We heard heavy boots on stone steps, heard the coarse laughter of half-drunk men. We scattered among the shelves of wine. I stood with my back to a row of dusty bottles, hoping I wouldn't knock one loose and give away my position.

Four guards with rifles slung over their shoulders bounded into the cellar and began to examine bottles on the nearest shelf. I could see Uturo in the aisle next to mine, but the other warrior and Elicia were out of sight. I held my breath and waited.

"This is the cheap stuff, for the neophyte monks," one of the guards snarled. "Look around and find the bottles reserved for our esteemed leader."

They started looking around, coming closer and closer to the aisles where Uturo and I were hiding. I kept wondering where Elicia and the other warrior were hiding, hoping the guards wouldn't stumble across them first.

I didn't have to worry about that. The guard who'd complained about the cheap stuff was heading directly for my aisle. I moved down a few feet, to position myself out of range from the other three guards, held Wilhelmina at the ready and waited.

He turned into the aisle and I squeezed the trigger. I saw a portion of his head blow away, saw the smile of anticipation turn to one of horror. In the quiet cellar, the boom of the luger was like a dynamite blast.

In that same instant, Uturo stepped from his aisle and began shooting at the other three guards. Another automatic rifle from the right began to chatter. Two other guards fell and I stepped out of the aisle to see the fourth guard charging up the stone steps toward the guard station. I aimed and fired, but he disappeared behind a wall. I was certain I hadn't hit him.

"Come on," I yelled. "Let's go before they gather their senses."

Knowing that we had been pressed into acting too soon, long before Sagacio could have done us any good, we went charging up the steps.

I was fully prepared for a fullscale shootout with the remaining guards at the station. As I neared the top of the stone staircase, I looked back to see that Uturo and the other warrior were right behind me. Elicia was nowhere to be seen and I had a kind of gut fear that perhaps she'd been hit by a stray bullet. There had been an awful lot of shooting down in that wine cellar.

At the top of the stairs, two doorways led off a narrow corridor. There was a torch burning in a holder at the end of the corridor and, near one of the doors was the fourth guard, crumpled up like a piece of foil.

I had hit him with that last shot as he had rounded the corner of the staircase. He had made it this far and had died before he could warn the others. And the winecellar was so deep and so well insulated with stone that the shots apparently hadn't been heard in the guard station. I held up my hand to stop the charging Uturo and his friend.

"Time for a bit of discretion instead of foolhardy valor," I said. "Let's go below and set up a plan. Uturo, grab an arm and let's take this dead guard with us."

Quietly, we retreated, dragging the dead guard down the staircase into the cellar. Wine from broken bottles now covered the floor. I called out to Elicia, but got no answer. Time was running out for us, but still I made a quick search among the aisles. No Elicia. I was starting down the corridor toward the arsenal when footsteps sounded on the stone staircase.

The warriors and I went into a defensive stance behind the racks of wine bottles. I aimed the luger at the base of the steps and waited, my finger itching to blast away at more guards. Sagacio's bulky frame appeared in my sights.

"Don't shoot," he said, gazing fearfully around at our leveled guns, at the four dead guards and at the broken wine bottles.

"What are you doing back down here?" I demanded. "You were to create a diversion among the guards."

"The station is empty," he said, the look of puzzlement back on his pudgy face. "I took the wine to Don Carlos and found him even more furious than ever. The storm has passed, but the whole of Alto Arete is still swathed in clouds. The wind seems to have died and the clouds aren't moving away. The signal wouldn't be seen. If they don't clear soon, Don Carlos will use his radios to call for the revolution."

"That means we don't have any time to fool around," I said. "We'll put on the uniforms of the dead guards and you can lead us out of here. Do you know where the guards are—the ones from the guard station?"

"I have no idea. When I returned from the palace and found the station empty, I thought perhaps you had killed them all. These four," he said, indicating the dead guards whose uniforms we were stripping, "aren't on duty now. They must have found the station empty and come down to steal wine."

That much was obvious, but I was still puzzled by the absence of guards at the station. And I was worried about Elicia. But, again, I thought, there's no time for anything but action. We donned the uniforms of the dead guards and, with Sagacio going ahead to make certain the way was clear, we went up the steps again.

The guard station was indeed empty. I checked the cabinets of rifles, grenades and mortars, pocketed a couple of grenades, and peered out into the courtyard.

In the dim distance, the palace loomed like a fairyland castle in swirling fog that was the immense cloud resting on top of Alto Arete. Lighted torches fought vainly against the darkening cloud, but I could see the main gate of the palace, see that no guards stood in the courtyard or near the gate. I opened the door leading to the courtyard and held up my hand as a signal to those behind me.

"Sagacio, you take the lead. When you're half-way across the courtyard, we'll follow."

The chubby monk took one fearful look at the empty courtyard and the swirling fog, hitched up his smock and marched through the doorway. I watched as he strode across the cobblestones and wondered where he was keeping the Russian rifle I had given him earlier.

The shot rang out clear and loud, only slightly muffled by the thick cloud. I looked around to see where the shot had come from, but it was dark and silent out there. When I looked back Sagacio, he was stopped in the center of the courtyard, his face peering up through the cloud at the upper stories of the palace.

Another shot came. I saw the pinpoint of flame this time. It was from the roof of the palace.

This time, Sagacio didn't merely stand in the courtyard. He turned toward us, his face writhing in pain. He held up pudgy hands in a kind of supplication, begging us to understand that he hadn't betrayed us. Then, he spiraled to the ground, his smock settling about his fat dead body like a shroud.

Even as I was feeling sorry for the hefty little monk and trying to decide what to do next, the rain of bullets began.

Thunder seemed to break out on the mountaintop. Bullets crashed through the windows of the guard station. The courtyard filled with rushing, running shapes, all firing rifles. At us.

A kind of hell had come to the mountaintop, and we were at the core of that hell.

CHAPTER TEN

The gunfire was murderous. It seemed that every gun in the possession of Don Carlos Italla was being aimed and fired at the guard station where Uturo, his fellow warrior and I were hiding.

All the windows were blasted into glass confetti in the first few seconds, and the rain of bullets were chipping away stone and splintering wood so fast that the station wouldn't be standing in another couple of minutes.

It was then, when the gunfire seemed at its peak, that I decided to act. I cradled an automatic rifle in my right arm, clutched Wilhelmina in my left hand, clamped Hugo in my teeth and, with a jerking motion for Uturo and his friend to follow, dashed into the courtyard.

It was the last thing the enemy expected. While all guns still blasted away at the empty guard station, we zig-zagged our way across the courtyard. Our guns blazed away at the pinpoints of fire indicating enemy gunmen. It was a suicide dash and we knew it, but remaining in the guard station was equally suicidal.

We reached Sagacio's body without incident, although I was certain that my luger had picked off at least two or three gunmen in the swirling cloud. From screams in other directions, I knew also that Uturo and his friend were having similar luck. They had come a long way from their fear of the cave's curse.

We regrouped in the center of the courtyard and I jammed a new clip into Wilhelmina and pointed toward the gate to the palace grounds.

"If we can make it inside, we may have a chance," I hissed through the blade of the stiletto. "They won't dare turn that withering fire on the palace itself. Let's go."

Bullets were already dancing in the courtyard when we started our final dash toward the gate. I emptied the automatic rifle and threw it away. I took the luger in both hands and, instead of firing wildly, began to pick out specific targets on the roof of the palace.

My first shot got results. A scream ripped through the muffling fog and I saw a man with ammo belts all over his body come tumbling down the side of the white stone building. He crashed into the bushes near the main door of the palace. Another shot and another heavily armed man plummeted from the roof.

And we were at the gate, all three of us still alive and still firing.

I skipped inside the gate and plunged behind a clump of bushes alongside the stone fence. I felt Uturo land just behind me. On the other side of the path, the other warrior took refuge behind a stone fountain. As I had expected, gunfire from other areas stopped immediately. We had only the fire from the roof to contend with.

I shoved in a new clip and methodically went along the roofline, picking off guards as I went. When five of them had fallen into the gloomy darkness at the front of the castle, the night went suddenly quiet.

There was no chance, though, that we had destroyed them all, or that we could expect those outside the palace to continue to hold their fire. The only thing to do, then, was the unexpected. They expected us to remain hidden inside the stone wall alongside the gate.

"Let's rush the door," I snarled. "Now."

Both warriors leaped to their feet, their rifles aimed and ready. We took two steps toward the door and I heard a whistling sound from above, felt a fluttering of the wind around my face. The net dropped so neatly into place that we were entangled in it before we even knew what was happening.

I was struggling to take aim on an immense tall guard who had opened the palace door when I felt the net tightening around me. I saw Uturo and his friend fighting the tightening net. I fired, but a sudden jerk of the net spoiled my aim and the bullet bounced harmlessly off the white stone of the palace wall. The net closed in, so tight now that it was cutting off circulation to my arms and legs.

A strand of strong nylon encircled my neck and I could feel it tightening even more. I was strangling. Even so, I rammed the luger between two strands and took aim on the huge guard standing in the open doorway. I was preparing to fire when the net jerked swiftly against my wrist and I found the luger pointing at the ground. The strand about my neck went tighter and I felt myself passing out.

"Leave go of your weapons," a voice boomed in the silence, "and the net will be released. Keep them and you will die of strangulation."

I tried to look around to see who was talking, but the net was cutting into my skin now. I couldn't move, and I could tell that Uturo and his friend had also stopped struggling. I heard their rifles clatter to the pavement. I tried once more to aim Wilhelmina at the guard in the palace doorway, but the breath of life went out of me. The stiletto fell from my teeth. I went momentarily unconscious, awakening to feel someone taking the luger from my hand.

Guards seemed to come from everywhere now. The net began to loosen and circulation began to return to my aching limbs. My neck felt as though someone had lashed it with a whip. As guards began to pull us from the net, the gigantic guard who had stood so brazenly in the open doorway began to walk down toward us. He got bigger and bigger as he came near.

I saw then that he wasn't merely tall. He was immense. I guessed him at seven feet in height, perhaps three hundred pounds in weight. And I could tell by his uniform that he was no mere guard. He had enough brass and medals on his cap and chest to have subdued a lesser man. Even before he opened his mouth, I knew who he was.

"I am Don Carlos Italla," he said, striding up to us and looking down with something akin to disdain. "Welcome to my humble abode in the clouds."

"Some humble," I muttered, sitting up and massaging my neck and limbs where the nylon netting had cut into them. "You've come a long way from Ninca land, Ancio."

The use of his original name had a violent effect on his face and body. He went rigid, drawing himself up to his full seven feet of height. His eyes narrowed and I saw the red glint in them, indicating remembered hatreds. In that moment, he was the epitome of the description given to me by old Jorge Cortez:

A giant of seven feet, a mountainous specimen of three hundred pounds, eyes like ingots of burning phosphorous, hands that could shred stainless steel slabs. A fury of a monster with a booming voice like the rumble of thunder.

The image faded when Don Carlos tried a smile. But only faintly. It came off like a caricature of Death regarding his next victim. His eyes, dark with the red glow still at their centers, flickered around at the assembled guards.

"You will henceforth refer to me as Don Carlos," he ordered. "All that Ancio business is in the past. I am no longer Ancio, no longer a Ninca. You will do well to remember that."

I was about to ask what the hell worse he could do to us if we persisted in calling him Ancio, but I got no chance. He snapped his fingers at the guards and ordered them to take us to his inner chamber. We were hustled to our feet and, even though it was difficult walking, we weren't given a chance to dawdle. I rambled along on aching legs, down corridors, up sweeping staircases, through spacious galleries and, finally, into an honest-to-goodness throne room at the rear of the palace.

If nothing else, Don Carlos had good taste in decor. The parquet and mosaic marble floors were enhanced by colorful Persian rugs that would have gone for a fortune in New York or Washington. The white marble walls were graced by original paintings by Dega, Monet, da Vinci, Michelangelo, Manet, de Vriess—even a few Picassos. Silk draperies covered every window and alcove.

The throne room was immense, befitting its main occupant. Persian rugs, draperies, paintings and fluffy pillows were everywhere. The throne itself sat on a marble pedestal. It looked like a monument to hugeness and importance, yet it had enough silk and velvet upholstery to look almost gentle.

Behind the throne, on a section of wall between two doorways to open balconies, hung da Vinci's painting of The Last Supper. For a moment, I was convinced that it was the original, but I knew that the famous painting actually was in the Vatican. It was, to say the least, the most precise and perfect copy imaginable.

Don Carlos took one hefty step to the pedestal and settled himself in his uniformed and decorated glory directly under the famous scene of Jesus and his disciples breaking bread for the final time. If Don Carlos took one hefty step to the pedestal and settled himself in his uniformed and decorated glory directly under the famous scene of Jesus were soft and compassionate; Don Carlos Italla's eyes still glowed with demonic intensity.

The throne room gradually filled with monks and guards, all keeping a respectful distance from the throne. Don Carlos had me, Uturo and the other warrior led to a small couch directly below his pedestal. We had to crane our necks to look up to him, and that was what he wanted.

"And now, Mr. Nick Carter," Don Carlos said in that booming voice of his, "I must say that I'm pleased you weren't killed during your foolish journey to my humble abode. Oh, I have known of you for some time, ever since your imperialistic masters placed you on the sacred soil of Nicarxa. I have kept track of your exploits with interest. I have issued orders for your death, and have executed many who have failed to carry out those orders."

He took a breather then, belched a few times, swigged from the bottle of wine Sagacio had recently brought him, and glared down at me with those fiery-red eyes.

"Now," he said, settling back in his velvet-padded throne as though he had a long and interesting tale to relate, "I must say that I had begun to engender a certain amount of respect for your skills and for your persistence and for your successes. But you were doomed from the beginning. You see, I knew that if all else failed you would somehow find the natural chimney leading up from the sacrificial cave. On the off chance that you would succeed in reaching and breaching my wine cellar, I was prepared for that. I knew of Sagacio's penchant for trying to remove that stone from the wall leading to the chimney. I was aware also of the efforts of his fellow tribesmen to use that as a route of escape. I sent Sagacio for wine at just a time when I knew that you would be at the mortared stone, if you, indeed, had succeeded in traversing the chimney.

"I would like to say that Sagacio, in the end, betrayed you out of loyalty to me. But I am a religious man, Mr. Nick Carter. Truth is important to me. Sagacio betrayed you, but not out of loyalty to me. He betrayed you by the look of ecstasy on his face when he brought me this final bottle of wine. I knew then that he had located you and had let you into the wine cellar.

"It was then that I let him return to you, but not before I had ordered the guards to vacate the guard station and set up positions in other areas to annihilate you and your friends—my former fellow tribesmen—when you emerged from the wine cellar. As I said, you were doomed to failure from the beginning. But I have one question, Mr. Nick Carter. There was a woman with you, a girl, actually. There were others, including Pico the old hermit and Purano, the son of Botussin. There were other warriors as well. Might I prevail upon you to tell me what has happened to them?"

I told him about our journey to the cave entrance, our battle with his guerillas, the killing of eight of our warriors, the wounding of Purano and Pico. I told him of our ordeal with the bats and how the first warrior had fallen to his death when the bats attacked him. I told of how the second warrior had been killed when he encountered the nest of scorpions, of how I had eliminated the scorpions and had eventually found the square stone and had loosened its mortar.

"And the woman—the girl? I believe her name is Elicia."

I had told him the truth all along. I saw no reason to tell him that Elicia was still at large, perhaps in the winecellar. Besides, I still had the ominous feeling that she had been killed in that exchange of gunfire with the wine-stealing guards. When I lied

to Don Carlos, it was only a half-lie. I believed it to
be *possibly* true.

"She died when four guards entered the
winecellar to steal your wine," I said. "There was
gunfire and a stray bullet killed her."

He stared at me for a long moment, then made a
small gesture with his right hand. I noticed that he
had huge diamond rings on each finger, including
his thumb. I turned and saw that a guard was leaving the throne room.

"If you speak true," Don Carlos said, "the girl's
body will be located and brought up for burial. We
are not animals here, Mr. Nick Carter." He got up
and went down the back side of his pedestal. He
opened the drapes to a balcony and stepped
through. He was gone for only a few seconds, then
returned with a wicked smile on his broad face.

"The clouds are clearing away," he announced.
He snapped his fingers at an old monk who stood
nearest the throne. "Fetch the case bearing the
flares and flare gun," he ordered. "In a minute or
two, the clouds will be gone and I shall send the
signal. The battle is long overdue."

"I don't suppose," I said, trying to decide whether to set off one of my gas bombs and wiping out
everybody in the throne room, including myself,
"you'd like to discuss sending that signal, would
you?"

Don Carlos stared at me for a long time, his face
impassive, his eyes only barely glowing red in the
centers. Then, obviously convinced that I was making a joke, he leaned back in his throne and let out
a series of guffaws that actually made the painting
of The Last Supper rattle against the wall. There
was dead silence from the monks and guards be-

hind me. Apparently, when Don Carlos laughed, he laughed alone, unlike other bosses who insisted that underlings share their warped sense of humor. Don Carlos finally wound down and the famous painting stopped rattling against the wall.

"Along with everything else," the fanatical giant said, his face set like cement, his eyes glowing again, "you have an abominable sense of humor, Mr. Nick Carter. There is, of course, nothing to discuss. My people await the signal and I'm certain they've grown impatient by now. We will not even discuss what is to happen to you, to your two Indian friends and to those others on this mountaintop who have continued to show disloyalty to me. Once the revolution commences below, all of you will be dispatched. In case you are interested in the method, it will be a simple death. You will all be thrown from the summit of Alto Arete. If the fall doesn't kill you, the poisoned bits of metal will rip your flesh to shreds when you try to descend. If you survive that, Cuban Marines await you below. This time, no miracle and no ally will come to your rescue. Ah, the signal flares have arrived."

The monk bringing the leather case containing the signal gun and flares approached the throne, bowed and handed the case up to his master. I entertained a faint hope that the man was a Ninca, one of Sagacio's friends, and that he had booby-trapped the damned case. But that wasn't to be. Don Carlos opened the case and took out the flare gun. I naturally wanted to stall him as long as possible, not knowing what a stall would do to help, but there was something else that bothered me. Something the President had told me when he had sent me on this assignment. "There's a rumor that someone in the country once did something rather atrocious to him or to his family." I had asked Chief Botussin about it, but he had no knowledge of anything atrocious ever having been done to Don Carlos. I had to find out the story there—I hate dying with a mystery lingering in my brin.

I asked Don Carlos Italla about it. He slumped back in his throne, the flare gun on his lap, the case of flares beside him.

"You are the first man who has shown an interest in that travesty of justice," he said. "The clouds haven't fully cleared, so I will take the time to reply."

When he was sixteen, he said, his voice getting tight as he remembered, he and a group of his Indian friends went into the capital to see the sights. There, because he happened to smile at a young woman (not an Indian), a priest who was half drunk slapped him around until his face was bloody. Police and others stood by and watched, then chased Ancio and his friends from the city.

"I developed then a hatred for all Indians because the persecution stemmed from the fact that I was Indian. I developed a hatred for non-Indians because they were the ones doing the persecuting. But I learned an important lesson about the power of priests, of holy men. I decided to become a priest and to someday avenge the wrong that was done to me, the shame that was put upon me in the presence of my friends."

He stopped and I waited for him to go on. But that was it, the whole bag. All this—this whole bloody revolution and all the killing that had already taken place, plus the distinct threat of a third world war—had come about because a 16-year-old boy had been flogged by a stupid and drunken priest on the streets of the capital. That event had festered in the brain of this evil giant. Nothing atrocious had happened to the young Ancio, except in his own mind, and I knew that no power on earth could reverse the course of that demented mind.

"Detain them while I give the signal," Don Carlos said, standing suddenly and stepping from the throne. "If they so much as move an eyelash to stop me. . ."

He got no further. A thunderous explosion ripped through the bowels of the earth beneath us. The whole palace shook like a treehouse in a hurricane. The painting of The Last Supper clattered to the floor. Vases and goblets and other knick-knacks crashed and shattered on the marble floors all around us. The silk draperies flapped in the breeze.

Don Carlos was still standing there, looking puzzled, when a second explosion came. It ripped up through the front of the throne room, near the door behind Uturo and me and the other warrior. I turned to see the door itself disappear in a pillar of rising flame. The guards and monks standing there were knocked about like pins in a bowling alley, their clothing on fire.

I spun back around in time to see Don Carlos disappear through the draperies to his balcony. I leaped onto the pedestal, dashed past the throne, jumped down the other side and was through the drapes just as Don Carlos had primed the flare gun and was raising it above his head.

As he had said, there was nohing to discuss anymore. I didn't say a word, not even a shout or a grunt. I made a flying leap, hit the giant squarely in the back and felt us both plunging forward against the low outer wall of the balcony.

In seconds, we were flying through space. The main thought in my mind was that it was no longer foggy. The clouds were indeed gone and that flare would have been seen all the way to Florida. I hadn't given a single thought to what might have caused that explosion, but it couldn't have come at a better time. My main interest, in that moment, was to land in such a way that I didn't break every bone in my body.

Fortunately, the throne room was on the second floor at the rear of the palace. There was a soft flower garden below instead of a cobblestoned courtyard. And I landed smack on top of Don Carlos. That excess fat around his middle not only provided a cushion for me, but kept him from being killed in the process.

For a big man, he was swift. He lay on the ground no more than two seconds before he was up, the flare gun raised again. I had no weapons other than the gas bombs. So I rushed him again and reached for the outstretched hand holding the flare.

Don Carlos saw me coming. He lashed out and swept me aside like a pesky gnat. I quickly regained my bearings and took dead aim on the middle of his back. I hit him with all my strength, my legs churning like pistons. Don Carlos let out a bellow of rage, but my charge had the desired effect. I pushed him halfway across the garden and made him lose his grip on the flare gun. The gun flew toward the rear wall and landed beside an open gate. It was dark beyond that gate, but I knew from

Luis Pequeno's description of the mountaintop that the gate opened up to a narrow ledge overlooking a sheer drop of a thousand feet.

Don Carlos ignored me now, and rushed headlong toward the gate and the flare. He still carried the case with the other flares and I wondered why he was so protective of it. I rushed after him. We both reached the gate at the same time. Don Carlos started to stoop for the flare gun, saw me rushing toward him, and lashed out with the flare case.

He caught me square in the face and I went down at his feet like a rock. I felt woozy, but turned over in time to see him bringing the case down in a slam that would have knocked all the juices out of my head. I spun over on the ground and Don Carlos struck a spot where my head had been. The case broke open and two flares popped out onto the ground. They rolled through the open gate and lay near the edge of the mountain.

"You bastard," Don Carlos swore. "I will make your death a slow and painful one for this."

He kicked out at me, but the blow was a glancing one. I was starting to my feet when Don Carlos dashed through the gate to retrieve his errant flares. Why was he so protective of those damned flares when he had the loaded flare gun in his hand? He could send the signal anytime he pleased.

No matter, I thought. Stop him while he's preoccupied with those extra flares. I rushed through the gate, careful to time my leap so that I didn't go over the side of the hill with the giant. Don Carlos was stooping over, his hand scooping up one of the flares, when I hit his wide buttocks with my shoulder.

He stumbled forward, both hands outstretched,

a flare in one hand, the flaregun in the other.

I waited, knowing that he had lost his balance and was teetering on the edge of the precipice. Even as his arms were windmilling, trying to regain balance, I heard a staccato burst of gunfire from beyond the palace. Obviously, Uturo and his friend weren't idle during this critical time. I hoped they had recruited enough fellow tribesmen whose hatred for Don Carlos overcame their loyalty, but that might be too much to hope for.

Right now, it looked as though Don Carlos was winning his war with balance. He was doing less windmilling with his arms. He was about to settle back on his heels, safely back from the ledge.

I paused only a short time, considering letting the man live now that he was obviously losing this battle in the clouds. But I had learned from bitter experience that an enemy is never vanquished by those who show premature mercy. If he fired that flare, it would be all over, no matter what happened up here.

I reached out and gave him a push. A hard one.

He went over. A combination scream, bellow and final order burst from his lips, but not even the fates were any longer listening to orders and appeals from Don Carlos Italla.

It was all over, I thought.

And then I heard the soft whoomp and saw the flare arc high in the dark sky. Even in his moment of death, Don Carlos had sent the signal for the bloody revolution to begin.

Damn, I cursed myself. I shouldn't have pushed him, not yet. I should have yanked him back from the precipice, wrestled the flare gun from him and then pushed him over. But then, I decided, I might not have had the option. He might have prevailed in the battle over the gun, pushed me over the side and then sent the signal.

With a sick feeling, knowing that bloodshed had already begun far below as a result of Don Carlos's signal from Alto Arete, I turned back to the palace. I had no weapon, except spare gas bombs, but I fully expected to pick one up from the first dead man I came across. I hoped against hope that that first dead man wouldn't be Uturo or his friend, or anyone else friendly to our cause.

At the side of the palace, I found a dead guard, one I had shot from the roof earlier. I took his rifle and ran to the front of the palace. Sporadic gunfire was taking place in the courtyard and I rushed up to the porch for a better view, ready to add to Uturo's gunfire.

I wasn't really needed just then. As I searched the courtyard for an enemy to shoot, I saw several guards emerge from a barracks with their hands up. They were shouting:

"Stop shooting, stop shooting. We give up."

Other guards emerged from bushes and from behind stone fences around the courtyard. When a couple of dozen of them had assembled, still holding up their hands, Uturo, his fellow warrior and a number of armed monks emerged from other buildings. Uturo had found the friendly monks without Sagacio's help.

We had won the war on top of the mountain, but it must be a far different story down below, in Nicarxa. And I was certain that I had lost Elicia, that she had been killed in that exchange of gunfire with the wine-stealing guards. If not that, she'd been killed by the guard Don Carlos sent to find her. If not that, the explosion surely had torn her to shreds.

I had already guessed that the explosion had come from the arsenal alongside the wine cellar. Why it had been blown up, I didn't know, but I did know that anyone in or near that wine cellar had to be a sure goner.

There was no feeling of victory as I marched into the courtyard where Uturo and his friends had rounded up all the guards who had remained loyal to Don Carlos. They all turned to look at me.

"Don Carlos Italla is dead," I whispered to Uturo, "but he lived long enough to send the signal. I'm afraid our victory up here is only temporary. Unless we can convince these people otherwise and keep the word to ourselves that Don Carlos is dead. In time, maybe we can use his headquarters in the clouds to mount a counter-offensive and throw out the Cubans. It'll be a ticklish business, though."

Uturo looked as defeated as I felt. He eyed the collection of guards in the courtyard and shook his head sadly.

"Such a good fight," he said sadly. "We did well, under your leadership. And it goes for nothing."

While we were standing there trying to figure out what to do next, the door to the guard station opened and a whole group of monks came strolling out. I recognized them as the religious followers of Intenday, the fanatic from Apalca, Don Carlos Italla's ally.

Uturo spun around, preparing to shoot the monks, but I stopped him. I don't know why—a feeling, a hunch. I had seen a familiar figure behind the monks, and that figure was carrying a Russian automatic rifle. That figure had herded the monks outside. That figure was Elicia.

My heart took an extra leap when I finally recognized her. I strode around the assembled monks and went to her side.

"I thought you were dead," I said. "My God, how did you come out of all that alive? How did you capture these Apalcan monks? How . . ."

"In time, Nick," she said. "Right now, I think I'm going to faint."

She was true to her word. She passed out even before the last word had passed her lips. I caught her and carried her into the guard station. I put her on a bullet-riddled couch and looked around for something cold to put on her forehead. She was as pale as death and I was about to tear off her clothes to look for wounds when Uturo and the Apalcan religious leader entered the guardhouse.

"This man says he has something important to tell you," Uturo announced. "He is Intenday. Perhaps we should listen to him."

I looked up and saw the wiry little man with the brown bald head and enormous eyes. There was no mistake; this was Intenday, the Apalcan religious leader I had seen that morning on the trail when he had come out of his tent for breakfast. I gazed past him, at his fellow monks and, sure enough, there was the fat monk who had been the fellow fire-tender of Nuyan, the man I had killed to infiltrate the ranks of the monks. He didn't seem to recognize me, but then how could he? He had never seen my face.

Intenday was a man who still stood on ceremony. As I rubbed Elicia's wrists to bring circulation around, he stood regally at the head of the couch and spoke in a soft, measured way:

"We had reached agreement with Don Carlos to commence the holy war at sundown and to purge both our nations of corrupt leaders. I thought it the best way—the only way—to accomplish what all holy men desire. I sought an end to corruption, to disease, to poverty, to tyranny. I believed I was right. I believed Don Carlos Italla was right."

"That's the trouble with this world," I said, rubbing Elicia's arms and peering anxiously into her too-pale face. "Everybody thinks their side is right and they always resort to the wrong ways to prove it. And Don Carlos was a worse tyrant than the men who now rule Nicarxa and Apalca."

"This I learned too late," Intenday said. "When I knew just how much of a monster Don Carlos really was, it was too late to change my mind about the agreement. We became his prisoners here on the mountain and against our will he was to send the signal that we were in agreement. But you must know . . ."

Elicia stirred on the couch and I held up a hand to shush the rambling religious leader. I was no longer interested in what he had to say. It was too late for that, too late for anything but to try to survive on this mountain while bloodshed reigned below.

"Elicia, come out of it," I said, slapping her face gently. Her head rolled back and forth and I saw faint color returning to her cheeks. My heart leapt for joy, but it was muted joy, knowing that her people below—and all the Ninca Indians—were being massacred by the hundreds.

She came around slowly and finally sat up on the couch. Intenday, still standing on ceremony, retreated a few steps, but stood implacably with his arms folded, his face clearly revealing that he had more to say and wouldn't leave until he said it.

"I'm sorry for fainting," Elicia said in a soft voice. "I meant to be strong, but so much had happened. I couldn't help it."

"What happened to you?" I asked. "How did you come through all this alive? And the explosion. . ."

Elicia interrupted me by holding her finger across my lips. That finger, dirty as it was from her ordeal, tasted sweet to me.

"I will tell you, slowly. First, a drink. I need something to drink."

Uturo brought a bottle of wine from under his shirt and, with a wink, popped off the cork. Elicia took a long draught and sat up straighter on the couch. We all listened to her story of terror and eventual success.

When the four guards had come to the cellar to steal wine and we started the shootout with them, Elicia had dashed into the corridor leading to the arsenal. She found the door open and dashed inside. When she closed the door behind her, it jammed in place and she couldn't get out again. She had banged on the door until her hands were raw, but we hadn't heard a thing.

The air in the closed arsenal was scarce and she began to gasp for breath as the minutes went by. She was nearly unconscious when the door finally opened. It was opened, I knew, by the man Don Carlos had sent to find her body.

"When he saw that I was alive and not wounded," she said, a catch in her voice, "he decided to take me, the way those Cuban Marines had been taking me before you came along to save me. He said Don Carlos was ready to send the signal, that the clouds had gone away, and that you and Uturo and Niko were prisoners."

"Niko? Who's Niko?"

"The other warrior," she said. "Uturo's friend. Anyway, he said it was all over for us and he might as well enjoy my flesh one more time before Don Carlos threw us all over the mountain. Oh, Nick . . ."

She started to cry and I massaged her hands and told her to take it slow and easy. She took another swallow of wine. Intenday moved a step closer, seeming ready to speak again, but I held up my hand to stop him. Elicia went on.

"I fought this man," Elicia said. "He was strong and I was nearly dead from lack of air, but I have been abused enough by animals. I fought as I have never fought before—as I *should* have fought when the Cuban Marines came. He nearly overcame me, but I got his gun away from him and killed him.

"I knew there wasn't time to rush to the palace to save you and Uturo and Niko, even if I could have done so. But I had to do something. I remembered looking at the map you had drawn of the fortifications. I remembered that the arsenal was directly under the rear of the palace."

"So you blew up the arsenal," I said. "How on earth did you do that?"

"I used the nylon rope you used to bring us up the chimney," she said. "I soaked it in brandy and ran it along the floor of the wine cellar and up the steps to the guard room. After I had lighted the fuse and was hiding in the guard room, the explosion came and I saw fire shooting from the top

of the palace. I thought I had killed all of you. And
then more shooting started in the courtyard and
this man, this Apalcan religious leader, and his
monks came rushing into the guard room for protection. I still had the gun I had used to kill the
man who had found me in the arsenal, so I held
them at bay until—until . . ."

She passed out again, more from the wine than
from exertion. I eased her back on the couch to let
her sleep this one off. She would wake up soon
enough. She would wake up to the horror of knowing that her countrymen were being slaughtered in
a useless revolution begun by a maniac.

I looked around the destroyed guard station, at
Uturo who still held the bottle of wine; at Intenday, the Apalcan religious leader who learned too
late that Don Carlos was a fiend. I shook my head
and muttered:

"So much waste. Such valiant efforts by so many
brave people and it all comes to waste. And there's
no way to stop it, is there?"

Intenday moved a step closer and I was prepared
for a sneak attack. He could have a weapon beneath that full red robe. Even though he'd confessed that he no longer was loyal to Don Carlos
Italla, he still had to be considered the enemy.

"There is no need," he said in a sing-song voice
of a man who has sung many prayers, "to stop
what has not even begun."

"I beg your pardon?"

"The revolution," he said. "It has not begun. In
fact, it will not begin. Already, the Cuban Marines
are starting their evacuation, and the insurgents are
surrendering to government forces."

I was skeptical, still watching his hands to make

sure they didn't snake a weapon out of his smock
while he had me off guard with his cockamamie
story about the revolution not having begun, about
the Cubans evacuating Nicarxa, about the sur-
render.

"Just how would you know all that?" I demanded. "Do you have a radio hookup to someone down below?"

"No," he said. "Nothing so sophisticated. Tell
me, how many flares did Don Carlos shoot into the
air above Alto Arete?"

"One," I said, "but you already know that. You
must have seen it."

"Yes, I saw it, and my heart rejoiced. I wanted to
explain to this young woman when she came in
here waving her weapon, but her eyes were so wild
and she was in no condition to listen."

"I'm in a condition to listen," I said. "Perhaps
you'd better explain."

"The plan," he said, "called for Don Carlos to
send up three flares if we were in agreement, if my
people in Apalca would join the revolution. Without my help, Don Carlos knew that he could not
succeed. Three flares, Mr. Carter, to start the
revolution. If there had been no agreement, Don
Carlos was to fire only one flare. One flare would
mean no support, it would mean defeat. But the
arrangement was only what you Americans call
window dressing. Don Carlos intended all along to
fire three flares, no matter what I and my group
decided."

"One flare meant it was all off?"

"Yes, but he intended all along to fire three.
I tried to dissuade him, but couldn't. When he
made us prisoners, I sent an emmisary to steal his

extra flares. The emissary was found and killed. Believe me, sir, I did all possible to halt the revolution. Now I find that it was halted quite by accident."

"No," I said, "not by accident." I was remembering how Don Carlos had scrambled for those extra two flares when his very life was in danger. I had wondered why he hadn't gone ahead and fired that damned flare gun. Now I knew.

"I didn't know the rules when I was out there butting heads with Don Carlos," I said, "but you can't convince me that what happened was an accident. Too many people were involved in stopping that man to call success an accident. Too many people died stopping him. Those deaths weren't accidental. Do you know what they were, what all this was?"

"No," the Apalcan religious leader said.

"Fate, my friend. You believed that God was on you side, that you were fated to win. Well, you lost, so take a lesson from it and don't get tangled up with fanatics like Don Carlos Italla again. And don't become more of a fanatic than you already are. If the people of Nicarxa let you out of the country alive, learn your lesson well, Intenday, and resolve your future problems with help from the God you say you believe in. And—oh, the hell with you."

"One thing I fail to understand," he said. "Don Carlos was a fanatic, devoted to this revolution. Why would he fire a single flare, knowing that it would signal the death of the revolution?"

I thought about that. The man was falling and knew that he would have no chance to fire two more flares, even if he had them on his person. Why, then, did he fire? Ah, it was simple.

"It was a case of the drowning man grasping at straws," I told Intenday. "Don Carlos was falling to his death. He would have grasped at anything to save himself. The gun was in his hands and, in panic, he clutched it and pulled the trigger. And I'm afraid that's about all the explanation we'll ever get because Don Carlos is no longer among us."

"Thank God," Intenday said, crossing himself.

I picked Elicia up from the bullet-riddled couch and walked out of the guard station into the square. The guards were sitting in a bunch in the center and the monks and Niko were still standing above them with guns. I walked past them and went up the steps and into the palace. A frightened servant approached, wringing his hands.

"Show me to the master bedroom," I said. "Give me ten minutes to get this lady on her feet, then bring us something good to eat and drink. After that, we're not to be disturbed. Is that understood?"

He nodded and dashed up the main staircase like a dog leading his master to the hunting grounds.

I knew I should be spending this time in another way. I should go directly to the radio room on Alto Arete and get a message out to AXE and the American President that the mission was completed, successfully. I should get a message to the Nicarxan president that his enemies had lost, that he could easily round up dissident guerillas at will. I should . . .

To hell with all that. The Presidents could wait.

One more night wouldn't make any difference to anybody in the whole wide world.

Except to me.

And to Elicia.

NICK CARTER

"America's #1 espionage agent."

—<u>Variety</u>

Don't miss a single high-tension novel in the Nick Carter Killmaster series!

☐ THE DAY OF THE DINGO   13935-3 $1.95
When a new agent turns up dead in Tokyo, Nick follows the trail of intrigue.

_____

☐ AND NEXT THE KING   02277-4 $1.95
Nick's mission takes him to Spain where a bizarre assassination plot hinges on a night at the opera.

_____

☐ TARANTULA STRIKE   79840-3 $1.95
KGB's top agent has been terminated — and Nick joins his beautiful replacement to find the assassin.

_____

☐ STRIKE OF THE HAWK   79072-4 $1.95
Two special Nick adventures in one volume.

Available wherever paperbacks are sold or use this coupon.

- -

C CHARTER BOOKS, Book Mailing Service
P.O. Box 690, Rockville Centre, N.Y. 11571

Please send me the titles checked above. I enclose $_____.
Include 75¢ for postage and handling if one book is ordered; $1.00 if two to five are ordered. If six or more are ordered, postage is free.

NAME _____

ADDRESS _____

CITY_____STATE_____ZIP _____

Ec